Dear Brio Girl,

Maybe you've heard that "God always answers prayer." But how do you respond when He doesn't answer immediately or He doesn't answer in the way you expect? Through Dragonfly on My Shoulder, you'll learn that's exactly where trust comes in. And for Solana that's especially hard because trust in God doesn't come easily for her. Can you identify? If you're ready to learn more than you expect, then you're ready to join Solana and the BRIO gang for another exciting adventure!

Your Friend,

Susie Shellenberger, BRIO Editor
www.briomag.com

BRIO GIRLS®

from Focus on the Family®
and
Bethany House Publishers

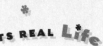

Hannah   Tyler   Becca   Jacie

Created by

LISSA HALLS JOHNSON

WRITTEN BY JEANETTE HANSCOME

BETHANYHOUSE
MINNEAPOLIS, MINNESOTA

Focus on the Family books are available at special quantity discounts when purchased in bulk by corporations, organizations, churches, or groups. Special imprints, messages, and excerpts can be produced to meet your needs. For more information, contact: Focus on the Family Sales Department, 8605 Explorer Drive, Colorado Springs, CO 80920; phone (800) 932-9123.

A Focus on the Family book.
Published by Bethany House Publishers
11400 Hampshire Avenue South
Bloomington, Minnesota 55438
www.bethanyhouse.com

Bethany House Publishers is a Division of
Baker Book House Company, Grand Rapids, Michigan.

Printed in the United States of America

Library of Congress Cataloging-in-Publication Data
Hanscome, Jeanette.
     Dragonfly on my shoulder / created by Lissa Halls Johnson ; written by Jeanette Hanscome.
          p.   cm. — (Brio girls)
     "A Focus on the Family book."
     ISBN 1-58997-088-8

CIP data is pending.

2003016757

Thanks:
To Norm, for so graciously accepting
the ups and downs of living with a writer.
To Christian, for loving characters that
he is too young to read about.
And to Nathan, for playing so nicely in the playpen
as I wrote many of these chapters.
And thanks to Kathy and the girls
for a fun research trip to the tattoo parlor.
What a learning experience!

chapter 1

In honor of my senior year, I want to do something WILD!

I must do something to recapture the old self—the true, sassy, extreme Solana. And I don't have much summer left to do it in.

Hey, journal. Do you hear my big sigh? Why did breaking up with Ramón suck the life out of me?

I suppose it didn't help that mi Brio familia took off on a three-week mission trip to Venezuela. Sure, I hung out with Kara. But it's not the same. And now, they seem a little different. But don't get me wrong, sweet journal—it's not like I wanted to go on the mission trip.

It's just that I feel left out of their new memories and friendships.

☺ Hey, Sol! What's with you? You getting weird and mushy on me? ☺

Yeah. Maybe I am getting weird and mushy. Must be senior year. College. Permanent separation from Copper Ridge. Toss in a little Ramón. Maybe it's all of that.

Astronomy camp at the end of summer will be a good distraction. As long as I can keep Dennis Sanchez away from me. Only one camp payment left. Then I'm off to discover a new lunar crater or something. Thanks to Tío Manuel and odd jobs around the ranch, I've been able to earn the dinero. If only Ramón wasn't working there so much. But one has to get beyond the past and grow up, right?

● ● ●

Solana stood in the shallow end of Becca's pool with Jacie and Hannah, her hands floating on the surface of the water. "Hey, Alvaro," she coaxed. "Try standing on the steps. We promise not to let you drown."

Alvaro clutched his Cheerios swim ring and backed up. "No, no, no."

Solana tried not to laugh at the scrawny seven-year-old. He'd prepared for a day of swimming with a raincoat and umbrella, along with his swim ring and Superman trunks. So far he hadn't put so much as one toe into the water.

She looked at Jacie and threw up her hands. "See? Kids hate me."

"Oh, and you try so hard to make them like you." Jacie grabbed a long neon-pink floating noodle.

"I *did* try."

"Let me show you how it's done," Jacie said, draping her arms over the noodle and splashing with her hands. "Look, Alvaro, it's fun. I'll hold on to you tight if you get in. The noodle will hold you up too." She let her legs and arms rise to the surface of the water as proof.

Let Jacie deal with Alvaro, Solana decided. She dunked herself under the refreshing water. *Why waste more time arguing with a kid? I came to Becca's to cool off, not to give a swimming lesson.* Solana opened her eyes underwater and watched Alvaro's and Jacie's cloudy, shimmering images dance over her head. When she was five she'd wanted to be a mermaid when she grew up. *I'm glad my friends don't know about that. I'd never live it down.*

She watched Tyler turn an underwater summersault until her lungs gave out. She popped her head out of the water—the muffled voices clear again.

"You can trust Jacie," Hannah assured Alvaro. She slid through the water and held her hand out to Alvaro, who took another step back. "Now, trusting Solana on the other hand . . ."

"Yeah." Jacie winked at Hannah. "You don't want to play with her."

"Hey!" Solana splashed Jacie and Hannah at the same time.

Hannah splashed Solana right back. Jacie jumped out of the way and shook her black curls.

"You look like a wet dog when you do that." Solana pushed a spray of water over Jacie's head.

Jacie smacked the water with her floating noodle, sending a spray into Solana's face.

All hands smacked the water, which flew in all directions. Alvaro shrieked, shielding his body with the umbrella. The splashing stopped instantaneously.

"Relax. It's *water*, not molten lava," Solana said under her breath, hoping that Alvaro didn't hear her. No matter how much she disliked children, she never wanted to hurt Alvaro's feelings. When she saw him she often thought of her childhood friend Marisa, who'd died of hepatitis in Mexico.

"Sorry, Alvaro," Solana, Jacie, and Hannah said in unison.

Becca back floated into the shallow end. "You guys, leave Alvaro alone. He'll get in when he's ready."

Alvaro picked up his stick horse and started to gallop around the covered patio area, still managing to hold his Cheerios ring and umbrella.

Hannah threw her head back, laughing. "Where's a camera when you need one?"

"Faster, Ramón, faster," Alvaro ordered the stick horse named after Solana's former boyfriend.

Hearing that name sent a jab into Solana's heart. Just then a hand grabbed her leg, yanking her downward. She gasped as Tyler burst through the surface of the water, growling like a sea monster.

Solana growled back, trying to hide the fact that he'd startled her. "Will you ever grow up?"

"Never!" Tyler let out an evil laugh and grabbed Solana's arm. "Race you across the pool. Four laps."

Becca leaned against the pool's edge and made bicycle-riding motions underwater with her long, athletic legs. "Go for it, Solana. You can beat him, no problem."

Solana lunged past Tyler, grateful for the perfect timing of his sea monster attack. He'd kept her from getting sappy about Ramón. She positioned herself against the edge of the pool, like an Olympic swimmer. "Prepare to lose, *mi amigo*."

"Come on, Jace," Tyler called. "Race with us."

Jacie shook her head. "I can't compete with you two. I'll watch the finish line for the winner."

"Wimp," Solana challenged.

"Yeah, you're no fun." Tyler laid his hands on top of Jacie's head and tried to dunk her, but she ducked out of his way.

"You race the loser," Solana insisted. "Meaning Tyler."

"Okay." Jacie hopped out and stood at the edge of the pool. Becca, Jacie, and Hannah yelled, "Ready, set, go!"

Solana and Tyler took off.

Solana swam for all she was worth. Becca and Alvaro cheered for her, while Jacie and Hannah rooted for Tyler. After the last lap, when she touched the edge of the shallow end, she raised her arms in triumph, only to see Tyler standing over her with a satisfied grin on his face.

"'Prepare to lose,' huh?" Tyler ran his hands over his sun-bleached hair.

Becca moaned as Hannah and Jacie cheered Tyler.

"Traitors!" Solana gave Jacie and Hannah an extra-mean scowl. "Now I know who my real friends are."

Before Solana had a chance to demand a rematch, Becca's mom came out with a pitcher and a stack of cups. Becca's older brother, Matt, followed with a plate piled high with cookies.

"Raspberry lemonade, fresh from the freezer!" Mrs. McKinnon announced, placing the pitcher and cups on the patio table.

"We have enough peanut butter chocolate chip cookies here to feed the whole neighborhood," Matt said. "So, knock yourselves out."

On her way out of the water, Solana leaned close to Tyler's face. "I'll get you next time."

"Poor loser," Tyler taunted.

The group gathered around the umbrella-covered glass patio table, all of them breathing in the heavenly combination of peanut butter and chocolate. Solana reached for a towel and squeezed her hair with it.

Tyler poured himself a cup of lemonade and gulped it down. "Ah! Refreshing after the big race. Winning sure takes a lot out of a guy."

"What's this? Your audition for the next Gatorade commercial?" Solana snapped him with her wet towel. "You can quit rubbing in your victory."

A hand tugged the shoulder strap of Solana's black two-piece and she whipped her body around. Jacie stood behind her, smiling.

"Nice suit," Jacie said, clearly trying to get Solana's mind off her defeat. "It's new, huh?"

"Not quite as revealing as some of your others," Becca said.

"*Becca*," Mrs. McKinnon scolded.

"It's a compliment," Becca insisted.

Solana searched for an answer to Becca's observation. The day she'd bought the suit she hadn't felt as drawn to clothes that left so little to the imagination. But how could she explain that to her friends when she didn't understand it herself?

"It was on sale," she told Becca. *That part is true.* "I plan to spice it up a little."

"How?" Tyler asked. "By cutting off the straps?"

"No, with a tattoo." She grinned. Until that moment, she hadn't known that's what she would do. But the idea had popped into her head. *Perfect!*

"A tattoo?" Becca wrinkled her nose.

Becca's mom and brother shook their heads. Their exchanged animated glances told Solana she hadn't shocked them a bit.

Solana tapped her shoulder blade. "Don't you think one would look good right here?" She tossed her hair. "Pilar got a rose tattoo for her birthday. But I won't get anything that common. I want something unique—something with meaning."

Hannah sipped her lemonade and sat in a patio chair. Solana expected her to say something about how sinful tattoos are, but Hannah stayed quiet.

Jacie reached for a cookie. "Your mother will never let you get a tattoo, Solana." She turned to Becca's mom. "Right, Mrs. McKinnon?"

Becca's mom shook her head and chuckled. "I'm staying out of this one." She walked back into the house. Alvaro dropped his umbrella and horse for a fistful of cookies and followed her.

"Just don't get a skull and crossbones," Matt said before snatching a cookie and following Alvaro.

"I'm surprised you didn't come home from college with one of those tattooed across your back," Solana shouted to him as he walked away. She smiled to herself, trying to imagine Becca's clean-cut brother sporting a giant tattoo under his Colorado Rockies T-shirt.

"Maybe next semester," Matt shouted back.

Becca plopped down beside Hannah. "If you're under 18, you need a parent's permission. And it has to be signed, in person, at the tattoo parlor. I heard some girls talking about it at school. So good luck."

Solana folded her arms and grinned in satisfaction. "I already have my mother's permission. When Pilar got hers, I said I might want one too. I was sure Mamá would have a fit. Instead she made me promise to let her know when I plan to do it so she can take me to a clean place. One of her cousins in Mexico went to a sleazy tattoo parlor and got an infection."

Jacie swallowed a mouthful. "I can't believe your mom's letting you."

"When she saw Pilar's rose, she admitted that it looked nice, that she doesn't mind tattoos as long as they're small and tasteful. I was like, this is Narina Luz talking?"

"My mom feels the same way about them," Jacie said. "Not that I'd get one. I'm not into pain or anything permanent. I'd only get one if I could change it depending on my mood or my outfit." She took a swig of lemonade.

Becca wrinkled her nose. "I don't want—"

Jacie's face lit up as she interrupted Becca. "Hey, Solana, can I design your tattoo?"

Ideas flashed through Solana's mind. "Would you? Really?"

"Jacie," Hannah piped in. "Why would you want to design something like that?"

Solana sighed. *Here we go. It's sermon time.*

"Why not?" Jacie asked, sliding down in the patio chair. Her curls dripped water, creating a puddle on the dimpled cement. "Tattooing is an art. As long as you're not putting an offensive symbol on your body, what's wrong with it?"

Hannah hesitated—not something she used to do. Since returning from Venezuela, she seemed less quick to preach. She swallowed hard then said, "Well, there's a verse in Leviticus that specifically says not to put tattoo marks on your body."

"That's Old Testament Jewish law," Becca said, laughing.

Hannah's brows drew together. She took a breath then carefully said, "There's also a verse in the New Testament about our bodies being the temple of the Holy Spirit. We aren't supposed to abuse our bodies. Jacie, if you design Solana's tattoo, aren't you encouraging her to do that?"

Solana snorted. "Abuse? I'm not talking about lopping off an arm."

"It's one little tattoo," Jacie argued. "Not much worse than getting your ears pierced."

Hannah slowly shook her head, deep in thought. "I just don't know."

"What if I got John 3:16 tattooed on my hip? Would that be okay?"

Everyone laughed except Hannah.

"I just don't think tattoos are right." Hannah looked at Tyler. "What about you? What do you think?"

Tyler put up his hand. "I'm with Becca's mom. I'm staying out of it."

He would have been on my side before his trip to California. Solana eyed Tyler. "Come on, Ty. I know you have an opinion. Spill it."

Tyler shook his head and reached for a second cookie. "No way. Tattooing is too much of a gray area for me. Sorry, Sol."

Solana let out a long, dramatic groan. "If it's a gray area, then it's not wrong."

"But that doesn't make it right either," Hannah corrected.

"The thing that bothers me about tattoos is that you can never get rid of them." Becca hiked up the shoulder straps on her swimsuit. "What if you wake up one morning and don't want it anymore? Or what about when you're old and your skin gets all wrinkly?"

"Yuck!" Jacie grimaced. "Solana, pick something that looks good wrinkled."

"Like a prune," Tyler suggested through a mouthful of cookie. "Or a raisin. Hey, Sol, how about that? You can have a little pile of trail mix tattooed onto your arm. You wanted something unique. Well, there you go."

"Oh, don't be stupid." Solana grabbed a cup and poured some lemonade.

The back door slid open and Becca's mom poked her head

out. "How many of you can stay for supper? I need to know how much hamburger to defrost."

"I have to work," Jacie said. "But thanks."

"I can stay," Tyler said. "Thaw about a pound for me."

"Pig." Solana moved in closer to him and snorted.

Hannah swallowed her drink. "I'm pretty sure I can stay too. I'll just need to call."

"I can't—" Before Solana could finish her answer a surge of panic raced from her chest, through her entire body. "Oh no! What time is it?"

Mrs. McKinnon looked at her watch. "Ten minutes to four."

Solana leapt from her chair and grabbed her towel. "I'm such an idiot! I can't believe I forgot." She pictured her Uncle Manuel, pacing in front of his large stable, checking his watch every few seconds, waiting for her to show up.

"What?" Becca sprang from her chair.

"I'm in big trouble." Solana frantically looked around for her tank top and shorts. "I promised Uncle Manuel that I'd help him this afternoon. I was supposed to be there at 3:30."

"Well, whatever it is, I'm sure he can handle it until you get there." Tyler handed Solana her clothes that had ended up tangled in a heap of towels.

Hannah reached under a nearby lounge chair for Solana's sandals and tossed them to her.

Solana shook her head. "He sold a horse. She's really skittish so I promised to help load her into the trailer and take her to the new owners."

"Do you want to call?" Becca's mom asked.

"No." Solana threw her clothes over her damp swimsuit and stepped into her sandals. "I better just leave. He won't start without me."

• • •

Solana pedaled her bike as fast as she could until she arrived at the gate leading to the back of Manuel's property. She slowed down a little, taking time to catch her breath and calm down. She wiped sweat from her forehead and looked around, hoping to spot the *tesoros puros*. Seeing them always mellowed her out. But in the hot weather they were nowhere to be seen.

She spotted the pond that marked the beginning of Manuel's ranch. She watched tiny specks in the sky above the water and surrounding grass—dragonflies, hundreds of them. Manuel's three daughters, Amelia, Victoria, and Rosa, had named it Dragonfly Pond years ago, inspiring their dad to name his ranch El Rancho de la Libelula—the Dragonfly Ranch. How many times had Solana and her cousins raced around the pond, trying to catch the darting winged insects?

Maybe I'll ride back down here later, she thought.

Once again, visions of an angry uncle brought Solana back to reality. She picked up her pace.

When Solana reached the house, she let her bike drop. "I'm here, *Tio* Manuel," she hollered as she ran toward the stable.

She waited for him to holler something back, or come out to meet her with an annoyed look on his face. Instead everything was quiet. Solana's heart sank. *Maybe he left without me.* She looked around. Maricella's car was gone but Manuel's sat in the dirt driveway. Manuel's new horse trailer was backed into the large circular corral.

"Manuel?" she called. "Sorry I'm late. I . . ." The sold mare galloped freely around the corral. The corral gate hung open. Amazed that the mare hadn't escaped, she hurried over to shut the gate and once more called for her uncle. Manuel's name was barely out of her mouth when she gasped. Her stomach jumped into her throat. "Manuel!"

chapter 2

"Why can't you tell me what's going on?" Solana pleaded with the nurse, hoping the woman could hear her above a screaming baby and a man with a deep, contagious-sounding cough. "I'm the one who called 9-1-1."

"I know that, but you're a minor."

Solana balled up her fists, wanting to punch something or someone.

"We called your aunt." The nurse reached for a clipboard. "I'm sure she'll fill you in when she gets here. Now, have a seat please." She turned her attention to the lady with the crying baby.

With a huff Solana sank into one of the brown vinyl-covered chairs. A moment later Maricella flew down the hall followed by Solana's parents.

Maricella rushed to the nurse. "I am here for my husband, Manuel Luz." She looked around, as if expecting to see him in the waiting area or down the hall. "Where is he?"

"The doctor is still examining him, Mrs. Luz." The nurse's voice was tender. Resentment boiled inside Solana. Why hadn't that nurse reassured her when *she* was upset and wanted to see Manuel? From the minute she walked in, the nurse had treated Solana like she was in the way. Solana glared at her.

Without acknowledging Solana, the nurse stood and patted Maricella's shoulder. "Try to relax, okay? I'll tell the doctor you're here."

Maricella nodded, fighting back tears.

Relax? Yeah, right. Solana's parents sat on the other side of Maricella. Mamá spoke soothing words in Spanish, assuring her that everything would be okay.

"What did they tell you on the phone?" Solana asked Maricella, desperate to know *something*.

Maricella took a deep breath and shook her head. "Only that Manuel had an accident at the ranch. They said they couldn't tell me more over the phone. Now I am here and still know nothing." Her hands flew up in frustration. A tear trickled down her pretty, smooth cheek and she brushed it away. With a trembling hand she dug through her purse for a tissue.

"I am sure they would have told you if it was life threatening," Solana's father tried to reassure Maricella.

"*Si.*" Solana's mother took Maricella's hand. "For now we will wait and pray."

Maricella's worry made Solana's heart ache. At that moment it hit her again—*this is my fault. If I'd been on time instead of fooling around with my friends . . .*

Maricella wrapped her arm around Solana and pulled her close. "I am so glad you were there, Solana."

Solana lowered her head and closed her eyes, sick with guilt. *But I wasn't there. Not when I should have been.*

"Tell me what happened, please." Maricella's voice and eyes pleaded, making Solana feel even worse.

Solana shook her head helplessly. "I don't really know." She explained how she'd found Manuel. Images of his unconscious, crumpled body and bleeding head made her stomach churn. "It looked like the horse had gotten spooked or something and trampled Manuel." She tried to gather the courage to tell her aunt that she'd shown up late. But the words stuck in her throat. She took a deep breath before trying again. "I was—"

"I'm Doctor Patterson." A tall man with graying hair stood in front of Maricella.

Solana's heart raced as she waited for Dr. Patterson's news, afraid he'd say Manuel was in a coma—or worse.

Everyone sat quiet, a heavy tension hovering in the air, while the doctor explained Manuel's injuries. Maricella and Solana gasped at the same time when they heard he had received internal injuries when the horse kicked him in the abdomen.

"At this point it isn't life threatening," Dr. Patterson explained. "He'll need surgery immediately though—abdominal *and* to repair torn ligaments in both legs. His left leg is also broken severely."

Solana sat dazed, like she was in a bad dream she couldn't wake up from. The horse had run over Manuel's legs. He also had a concussion and injuries to his back from being thrown backward. She only half heard the doctor explain the surgery her uncle would need. Her body ached for Manuel. She swallowed hard against the lump in her throat. The weight of her responsibility seemed to pull her down.

As the doctor left, Maricella turned to Solana's parents. "I should call Ramón," she said, hoarse from crying. "He should know what is going on."

Solana stood, almost involuntarily. "I'll be back." She took off down the hall before anyone could stop her or ask where she was going. Images of Manuel tormented her mind, along with thoughts of how much worse his injuries could have been if the horse had trampled his torso, or his head. The tears she'd fought back started to escape as she turned a corner and spotted a pay phone.

Maybe she should call Ramón herself. She could almost feel his arms around her, comforting her, stroking her hair. She pushed the thought out of her head. Why had she even considered the idea? Why was he still the first person she wanted to run to in a crisis? They'd broken up. She had just gotten to the point where she didn't dream about him every night. She could finally see him at the ranch and not cry over the cruel reality that they couldn't be together.

No.

She continued walking, watching the floor. Even if she could call Ramón, any sympathy that she got from him would stop as soon as he found out her role in the accident.

I need to talk to my friends, she thought. *They won't make me feel horrible for messing up.*

She searched the pockets of her denim shorts and was relieved to find a crumpled dollar bill and some change left over from going to the movies with Becca and Jacie.

"Hello." Becca's voice filled Solana with much-needed comfort. With tears drenching her face, Solana spilled the whole story.

"Solana, that's awful." Becca paused and repeated the news to the others in the room with her. "Tyler and Hannah are still here. We'll be right over, okay?"

"Okay." Solana grabbed a napkin someone had left by the phone and blew her nose.

The idea of seeing her friends lightened the weight on Solana's shoulders. *What would I do without them?* she wondered as she walked back to where her family waited. Even Hannah, who had annoyed her so much at the beginning of the school year, had become such a part of their tight circle that she actually looked forward to seeing her tonight—almost as much as Becca and Tyler.

When Solana reached the waiting area, her mother wrapped her arms around her. "You can see Manuel when the surgery is over," Mamá whispered. "You have been waiting here for so long."

Solana pulled away, shaking her head hard. "I'll wait until tomorrow. *Tia* Maricella needs to see him more. He shouldn't have too many people around anyway." How could she face Manuel? He was in surgery because of her. He'd be in pain and face months of recovery because of her. If Mamá and Maricella knew what she'd done, they wouldn't want her anywhere near Manuel. "My friends are coming. I'll wait for them outside."

● ● ●

Solana rubbed her bare arms as she walked with Becca, Tyler, and Hannah to a park across the street from the hospital. She missed the sunny presence of Jacie. Why did she have to work tonight?

"Do you want my sweatshirt, Sol?" Tyler offered.

Solana shook her head, even though the evening breeze was getting chillier. "I don't deserve to be comfortable."

"Stop torturing yourself." Becca led Solana to a weather-beaten wooden picnic table. "It wasn't your fault."

Tyler removed his gray sweatshirt and draped it over Solana's drooping shoulders. He sat across from her. "The accident could have happened no matter what time you showed up." He cocked his head, trying to make contact with Solana's downcast eyes. "You said yourself that the horse is skittish."

"You might have been injured too." Hannah's voice sounded motherly and sweet. "Maybe God allowed you to be late to protect you from that."

Solana looked into Hannah's tender eyes. She let out a sigh and shook her head. "Nice try, but that sounds a little far-fetched to me.

Why would God want to protect me when I was off playing instead of helping my uncle?"

She dropped her head into her hands. "Mamá expects me to be the first to visit *Tio* Manuel after his surgery. The idea of seeing him . . ." Unable to finish her thought, she let her arms fall onto the table. She traced a heart that someone had carved into the wood.

"You can't avoid him for the rest of your life," Becca said. "And I seriously don't think he'll blame you. Your uncle doesn't seem like that type of person."

"But *I* blame me." Solana's throat tightened.

Hannah lowered her face for a moment then looked at Solana. "When you see Manuel, just admit you feel responsible and ask for his forgiveness."

Hannah made it sound so easy—just waltz into the hospital room and say, "I'm sorry," like she was six years old and had accidentally broken a cheap vase in Manuel and Maricella's living room. How could "sorry" ever undo her mistake?

On the other hand, Becca had a point. She'd have to face her uncle eventually.

But how?

● ● ●

Solana pulled into a parking place and turned off the engine.

Tio Manuel, please forgive me for being late the other day.

She punched the steering wheel. She'd been planning her speech to Manuel for the past two days. Each version of it sounded lamer than the one before. She rested her forehead against the steering wheel and squeezed her eyes shut.

I can't put this off any longer. Her family was starting to ask why she hadn't visited Manuel yet. She'd run out of excuses. *Get in there,*

Solana ordered herself, *before your family starts to think that you just don't care.*

She opened the car door before the temptation to go back home got the best of her.

Twenty minutes later Solana sat rigid in the chair beside Manuel's bed and tried to think of something to say besides, "Hi. How are you feeling?" *Duh! How do I expect him to feel?* She clutched the small vase of flowers she'd bought in the hospital gift shop so tightly that she feared it would break in her hands. All she could do was stare at her uncle's tired, pain-pinched face, wishing that one of her relatives would walk in and save her from this awkward moment.

After what felt like hours, she cleared her throat. "So, where is everyone?" Evidence of the many family members who had rushed to Copper Ridge since the accident littered Manuel's room—newspapers, a Spanish edition of *People* magazine, empty coffee cups, someone's leather jacket.

"I kicked them out—told them to go get lunch or something." Manuel chuckled weakly. "Your *Tia* Yolanda brought me a plate of her award-winning enchiladas and tried to get me to eat. For her, food is the cure for everything. The nurse had a fit—said they were not on the menu for someone who just had abdominal surgery. No solid food for me for a while."

Solana forced an awkward, fake laugh. She rubbed a piece of baby's breath between her fingers and brushed away the tiny flecks that fell on her turquoise sundress. "Um. How are you doing?" *Grrr!!! So much for the speech.*

"As long as they keep the pain medicine coming, I feel pretty good."

She studied the red rose in the middle of her flower arrangement, trying to figure out what to say next. "Oh, here." She forced herself out of the chair and held her gift out to Manuel.

Manuel patted his bed and motioned for Solana to sit next to him. Like a child awaiting punishment, she walked over slowly. She set the vase on Manuel's bedside table. *Why doesn't he just blow up at me? I deserve it.* It hurt to look into his troubled eyes. *It doesn't matter what my friends say. I caused that pain on his face.*

"*Tio* Manuel," she said, before she lost her nerve again, "I'm so sorry."

He looked deep into her eyes. "Why are *you* sorry? Are you the one who trampled me?"

"You know what I mean. I shouldn't have been late. I promised to help get Sonrisa into the trailer. And it's not like I was late because I was doing something important. I was swimming at Becca's. I was totally irresponsible."

Manuel tried to pull his body up a little in the bed but gave up. "Solana, you're a kid. You lost track of time. Do you know how many times I got in trouble for that from my papá?"

Solana couldn't help smiling a little, picturing her uncle as a teenager, getting into trouble for the same things she got busted for.

"I got impatient." Manuel rested against the headboard. "I know better than to load a newly broken horse onto a trailer by myself. Especially one that spooks like Sonrisa."

Solana knew her uncle was right. Loading a horse like Sonrisa was one of the many jobs she'd been taught to always do in pairs. But still, she couldn't shake off the sense of responsibility.

"I should have waited for you," Manuel said before Solana could argue with him. He patted Solana's knee. Once again she saw a distant, sad look in his eyes. "So no more feeling bad. I made a mistake, okay?" He shifted his eyes from Solana's face and looked out the window, which had a depressing view of the brick building next door. He lowered his voice. "Now I must pay for it."

A flutter of relief went through Solana. Manuel didn't blame her. Still, she needed to do something to help him. "Well, you don't have to worry about the ranch while you're stuck in the hospital. I'll go over every day and care for the horses, or whatever needs to be done. My friends said they'd help too. I might even be able to get others to help."

Still looking out the window, Manuel sighed deeply. "That is nice of you, Solana. But there is no need."

"Well I'm going to. Ramón's a hard worker but he does have limits." She leaned over to kiss Manuel on the cheek. "So don't worry. We'll take care of everything."

● ● ●

For the first time since the accident Solana greeted her parents with a smile. She dropped the keys to her mother's car onto the kitchen counter and plopped into a chair.

"I saw Manuel." She reached for a cookie from a plate in the middle of the table. "He's obviously in pain but seems okay."

Her parents stared at each other across the table, saying nothing.

"What's wrong?" She looked from one parent to the other. "Manuel is going to be okay, right? I mean, the doctor said he would be."

"Manuel will be fine, *mi'ja* . . . but . . ." Solana's mother took her hand and squeezed it. She looked across the table at Papá. "We should tell her, Alessandro."

The sick feeling that had so recently lifted returned in full force.

Solana's father took a sip of coffee, then a deep breath. He gazed at Solana with sad eyes. "Manuel is going to lose the ranch."

chapter

"What?" Solana stared at her father, in shock. "It's not like Manuel won't recover. And he has plenty of us to help for now. I even decided not to go to astronomy camp. I called this morning and they're sending my money back."

"There's more to it." Solana's father gazed into his coffee cup. "Taking care of his horses and property is not the problem."

"What else is there?"

Papá ran his hands through his thinning hair. "The problem is money. Manuel took out a second mortgage last year to make some repairs and buy equipment. He had the payments all worked out. My brother would never borrow money he could not pay back. Well, then he had setbacks at the ranch."

"What kind of setbacks?" Solana tried to think back. "All I remember is a couple of horses getting sick."

"Sick horses mean vet bills," Papá said. "And sick horses don't sell. Don't forget his hay did not do as well this year, so there was less to sell. Now he has hospital bills on top of the loan and everything else. The doctor says he will need physical therapy, which means even more money."

Solana stood and paced back and forth in the kitchen. Why hadn't Manuel said anything to her about money problems? He had probably told Ramón. Why hadn't *he* mentioned something to her? As often as she helped at the ranch, why had they left her out of this? Or maybe she just wasn't paying attention. She should have somehow figured out that Manuel was living on the edge. And why had he insisted on paying her for all those extra jobs if he couldn't afford it?

She stopped mid-thought. "What about his medical insurance?" Maybe somehow in all the frenzy, her parents hadn't thought of that.

"It covers 80 percent of the hospital stay," Papá explained. "Even without the loan payment, 20 percent of his medications, procedures, and physical therapy are more than anyone can afford."

"Why doesn't the family get together and pay some of his bills for him?"

Mamá stirred her remaining bit of coffee, her spoon clanking hard against the mug. "You know we would help if we could. Everyone in the family would. *Familia* always helps each other out. But nobody has that kind of money."

Solana sank into a kitchen chair. Mamá was right. Her family wasn't poor but they sure didn't have much money to spare. Most of her relatives were in the same situation. They helped each other in hard times by bringing over homemade meals, doing household chores, and caring for a person's children. Even now Manuel and Maricella's ranch house was packed with their three daughters, *Tia* Yolanda, and her husband. She guessed that *Tia* Yolanda had taken over all the cooking and housework so that Maricella and her daughters could be at the hospital as much as possible.

"I can't believe this." Solana could barely get the words out. Once again guilt overtook her. Before she knew it, the dam burst, and the story of what happened the day of Manuel's accident poured out. "Manuel is losing the ranch because of me," she said through a flood of tears.

"No, Solana." Papá wrapped his arm around her. "He has been worried about losing the ranch for many months. He knew all it would take was one more big expense." He let out a long breath. "Of course he never said anything until now."

Mamá shook her head. "He is so proud." She patted her husband's shoulder. "Like all the men on Papá's side of family."

Solana got up and ripped off a paper towel to wipe her eyes. "This isn't fair. Whenever anyone in the family is in trouble, Manuel is the first one to jump in and help. Now when he's in a desperate situation, none of us can do anything."

She immediately thought of her favorite horses: Shadow and Carmen. Losing the ranch meant losing them. And the *tesoros puros*. Riding Manuel's horses on the trails behind his ranch was what allowed her to track the herd of wild mustangs. She'd met and fallen in love with Ramón at the ranch.

Her heart seemed so heavy that she almost felt unable to stand. Saying good-bye to Manuel's ranch would mean losing part of her life.

● ● ●

"Here you go, Sol." Tyler set a raspberry mochaccino—Copperchino's drink of the month—in front of Solana. "It'll make you feel better." He squeezed past a bookshelf to get to an empty chair in the corner of their favorite coffeehouse.

"Thanks, Ty," she whispered. She took a sip of the cool drink only because Tyler had bought it for her. Looking around at the other customers, she envied those who seemed happy and carefree. Did they understand what it felt like to lose a part of themselves?

"This can't be happening." Solana clutched the cup in front of her. "Manuel has worked too hard all these years to lose his ranch."

Jacie twisted the leather cord of her bond servant necklace—something she hadn't taken off since her trip to Venezuela. "Maybe he won't lose it. That's just the way things look now."

Hannah rested her cheek in her hand, eyes lost in thought. "He might come up with the money somehow."

"Like from a relative nobody has thought of," Tyler suggested.

"Right. Some long-lost rich uncle." Solana rested her folded arms on the table. "That's not going to happen." She balled her fists and punched the table. Her friends jumped. "I just wish I could do something. I mean, I thought I could help by keeping the ranch going. But that's not enough."

Becca sat up straight. Her face beamed with a big idea. "Maybe we can do more."

Solana looked across the table at Becca. "Do you have several thousand dollars lying around?" She tried hard to hold back her sarcasm. Becca was only trying to be encouraging. But Solana's comment still came out sounding sour.

"I wish," Becca said. "But we can *raise* some money for your uncle. People do it all the time. Our church just took a collection of over seven thousand dollars to help a family whose daughter needs heart surgery." She pulled her straw out of the smoothie and licked it. "Of course the family they helped goes to our church."

"My church has bake sales to help needy causes sometimes," Hannah said. "Maybe I can organize one. I have a great recipe for apple spice muffins. They're always a big seller."

Solana dropped her jaw. "You can sell a thousand dollars' worth of muffins? They must be pretty good."

"They are!" Hannah smiled then shook her head. "We'll sell

other things too, silly. That could be one of many fund-raisers."

"Hey," Jacie said. "We can have a slave sale!"

"Slavery is illegal in this country, Jace," Tyler teased.

Jacie swatted Tyler. "You know what I mean. We can sell ourselves as servants for a day, or sell our services—things we do especially well."

Solana took another sip of her mochaccino, leaning forward as she listened to Becca, Hannah, and Tyler throw out other ideas. Her head pounded with grief. But a spark of hope made its way to the surface.

Hannah reached into her purse and pulled out the small notebook that she used to record prayer requests. She flipped to the back of the book and began writing down the ideas they'd come up with so far.

"More ideas, people!" Hannah encouraged, looking around the table. "We can do this."

"How about a picnic basket sale?" Becca suggested. "You know, like the ones they have in cheesy old movies."

"Hey, don't make fun of old movies." Tyler flicked a straw wrapper at Becca. "What would you put in your picnic basket, Bec? Frozen pizza, boxed mac and cheese, and Twinkies for dessert?"

Becca shrugged. "Someone might like that, especially if you throw in a Mountain Dew. Besides, Nate will buy mine no matter what's in it."

Tyler leaned toward Hannah. "Scratch the picnic basket sale. We don't want to poison anyone." He rested his head against the wall behind his chair. "Hey, what about an art and music festival? We can sell Jacie's artwork—maybe auction it off or something. Hannah can sell her photography. Of course I'll provide the music."

He strummed an air guitar, smiling proudly, while Jacie and Becca exchanged smirks.

Solana rested her chin in her hands and thought about it. "That would be great, but it sounds a little complicated."

"Yeah." Jacie stirred her frozen latté with a straw. "It would take a lot of time to plan and pull off. We'd have to get permits and advertise—which would cost money."

Tyler's shoulders slumped in disappointment. "True."

"I don't think Manuel has much time." Solana slouched in her chair, exhausted from the emotional roller coaster of the past few days. "We need to come up with ideas that we can do *now*." She thought for a moment. *My astronomy camp money!* She told her friends about dropping out of camp. "I should get the money back next week. That will add $300 to the fund."

"Solana, no," Jacie insisted. "You worked really hard to come up with that money. Manuel wouldn't want you to drop out."

"He can't stop me. Besides, it's mostly his money anyway."

"But you've been looking forward to astronomy camp since before school let out," Becca reminded her. "It's the first thing that I've seen you get excited about since . . . well, for a long time."

"My uncle is worth it."

Hannah patted Solana's arm. "I'm sure he'll appreciate it." She added Solana's contribution to the list then flipped to the middle of her notebook. "Before I forget, I'm going to add this whole situation to my prayer list. I'll pray for wisdom as we decide on fundraising ideas, and also that we'll make the money your uncle needs. All of us have been praying for your uncle's recovery. I hope you don't mind, but my youth group is praying for Manuel too."

"That's fine." Solana shrugged. *Why don't I have a stronger urge to come up with the most sarcastic comeback possible, like, "Hey, while you're at it, pray for the fingernail that I just chipped"? I guess her sincere concern is just irresistible.*

Solana would never admit it, but she was actually glad for

Hannah's prayers. They couldn't hurt . . . and she was feeling desperate.

Before Hannah could make a big deal about her response, Solana anxiously rapped on the table with her fist. "Come on, girl. We're on a roll. Let's come up with some more ideas."

chapter 4

Feedback screeched through the karaoke microphone in Matt's hand.

"Tyler!" Solana yelled. "Turn down the sound before someone bursts an eardrum and sues us!"

Laughter trickled from the small crowd that had gathered in Becca's backyard.

Once Tyler had the sound cleared up, Matt continued his speech. "You may remember Jacie Noland as the grand-prize winner at last year's Copper Ridge Art Festival."

Jacie stood on a small makeshift auction block, grinning modestly as Matt summed up her artistic accomplishments. "And she has learned from the best, ladies and gentlemen. In March she attended the annual Professional Art Conference in Atlanta, Georgia."

Solana scanned the McKinnons' yard, amazed by how many

people had shown up for the servant auction. Becca and Kassy had invited most of their neighbors. Tyler, Hannah, Jacie, and Nate had brought friends from church and the Edge. Jessica Abbott and Damien had even shown up. The entire Connor clan was present, all scurrying around, looking for ways to assist. Tyra helped her brother, Tyler, with the sound. She and Kassy also volunteered to sell their baby-sitting services. Solana was the only one of her friends without family at the sale. She'd only invited Kara.

"I wish my parents could be here, to see all the support for Manuel." Solana unfolded a lawn chair and sat next to Becca under a shade tree. "But I'd rather surprise them after we raise piles of money." She smacked her forehead with the palm of her hand. "We should have videotaped the sale. Why do some of my best ideas come when it's too late?"

"Tell you what," Becca said. "We'll videotape the garage sale next weekend."

"That's hardly the same thing." Solana mimed holding a camera in front of her face. "Here's a customer, paying two bucks for my homecoming dress from last year. What a bargain! Oh, and look, Hannah's brother's old chess set sold. Suckers! It's missing a piece."

Becca pulled down Solana's hands. "Okay, okay, so it was a lame idea."

They turned their attention back up front.

"I bid 20 bucks for Jacie!" Damien shouted from the back of the crowd. Jacie covered a laugh, blushing as she smiled at the boy she'd once dated.

"Fifty!" A woman called from a chair near the pool.

Becca leaned close to Solana's ear. "That's Barb Neilson. She and her family live in that huge house on the corner—they're loaded!"

Solana listened more closely, as Barb Neilson and Damien tried to outbid each other. "Poor Damien. He doesn't have a chance."

"Two hundred dollars!" Mrs. Neilson shouted.

Becca clutched the arms of her chair. "Two *hundred?*"

Solana glanced back at Damien. He kicked the dirt in disappointment and shoved his hands into the pockets of his jeans. "I must admit, I feel sorry for the guy." She turned back to Becca. "But desperate times like these leave no room for sentiment."

Becca sneaked a quick peek at Damien. "I'm sure he understands."

"Going once!" Matt announced, holding up one finger. "Going twice." He paused and looked at Damien, who shook his head. "Sold to the lady in the navy blue dress!"

Solana laughed. "Bec, your brother is getting into this auctioneer thing way too much. He's starting to scare me." She waved and smiled at Jacie as she hopped off the auction block and made her way over to the lady who'd bought her. Kara ran up next and took Jacie's place on the block.

Becca made a face at her brother. "Matt's a wannabe actor today."

Hannah took an empty plate off the bake sale table and handed it to her brother Micah. "This is going great, Solana. The peanut butter cookies have completely sold out, and there are only three of my apple spice muffins left."

"Who made everything anyway?" Solana surveyed the table of assorted cookies, muffins, and brownies. A plate of homemade rocky road candy had sold out long ago. A thrill rose up inside her as she realized that each individual cookie represented money for her uncle.

"My family made most of the muffins and cookies," Hannah said, like it was something they did every day. "Becca's mom made cookies too, and the brownies. Jacie made the rocky road."

Solana shook her head in amazement. "That must have been a lot of work."

"Yeah, but it was fun work."

"I feel bad." Solana counted the remaining plates on the table. "I could have baked something."

Hannah removed plastic wrap from a new plate of brownies. "You've been busy at the ranch. Don't worry about it."

Solana watched Hannah. *She really is enjoying herself.*

"You should have seen the way stuff sold at the bake sale we had at last night's Edge meeting." Becca's eyes widened with excitement. "The food was gone in 20 minutes. We're planning another one for this week."

Solana plunked down 50 cents in front of Hannah and helped herself to a fudge brownie. "Just keep the chocolate coming and you'll always have customers."

Jacie scurried over, her face one big smile. "You guys, Mrs. Neilson hired me to paint a mural in her little girl's bedroom. Did you hear how much she paid?"

Becca slapped Jacie on the back. "When she sees the kind of work you do, she'll wish she'd paid more."

"Do ya think?"

"Of course!"

"Yeah, right." Jacie looked thoughtful. Like she hoped that was true.

"Your work will be seen by lots of other people, Jacie." Hannah handed two brownies to a tall red-haired boy. "—like the parents of that little girl's friends. Maybe you'll get to do more."

Jacie's eyes lit up. "That would be incredible."

"Just think," Solana said. "You helped my uncle and started a new business, all in the same day."

"What a story I'll have to tell when they interview me one day for *Entrepreneur* magazine." Jacie pointed toward the auction block. "Ooo! Tyler's up."

Becca scanned the crowd. She sat back and huffed. "And look who's right up front, waving her skinny little arm."

Solana craned her neck to see around a tall man in a cowboy hat.

"Twenty-five dollars!" Jessica called from the front row.

Solana scowled. "Figures." She stuck out her tongue in disgust. Would Jessica ever give up? *Tyler's way too good for her.*

Becca hopped up from her chair. "Jessica can't buy our Tyler."

Hannah nodded in the direction of the crowd. "Looks like she already is."

"She probably has her dad's credit card and can bid as high as she wants," Solana said. Then again, considering how much Jessica might contribute to Manuel's cause, maybe she could put her dislike of the girl aside for a day.

"Well, this sale is cash only." Becca took a step forward. "Forty dollars!"

"Where are you going to get $40, Becca?" Hannah asked. "Your video rental allowance?"

Becca put her hands on her hips and looked at the ground to think. Her head shot up in a moment of sudden inspiration. "We can pool our money. Come on, you guys."

Without hesitation Jacie dug into her pocket and pulled out a five-dollar bill. "I'm in! It's worth going without something this week."

The fun of the challenge suddenly took over the possibility of Jessica bringing in big bucks. Solana remembered a 10 that she had in her purse. "I'm in too."

Hannah sat on one of the ice chests behind her. "I'd contribute but I didn't bring any money. Sorry." She smiled and waved to Tyler. "This will be fun to watch though."

"Fifty dollars!" Jessica turned and smiled at Becca, Jacie, and Solana, obviously enjoying the competition.

"Seventy-five!" Becca enunciated each syllable.

Seventy-five? Solana grabbed Becca's arm. "What are you doing?

There's no way we have that much."

Becca looked around. She snatched the box containing the proceeds from that day's bake sale. "We have this!"

"No way!" Solana felt her heart skip a beat. Had Becca lost her mind? She reached for the cash box but Becca yanked it out of her reach.

Hannah jumped up, sneaked behind Becca, and snatched the box. "Becca! What are you thinking?"

"It'll still go to Manuel." Becca clasped her hands and pleaded. "Come *on!*" She turned to Jacie and grabbed her shoulders. "Jacie, back me up."

Jacie shook herself free. "Let go of me, loony." She looked at Tyler, standing on the auction block, and bit her bottom lip. "Oh, I hate to watch Tyler slip into Jessica's clutches, even if it is only for one day."

"Then help me get that box from Hannah before it's too late!" Becca made another move for the box but Hannah put it behind her back.

"One hundred dollars!" Jessica held up a one hundred-dollar bill, to show the crowd that she actually had the money.

"Show-off," Solana murmured.

Becca stomped her foot. "Great! I should have known she'd come prepared."

Solana crossed her arms. "Oh, let some Cadwallader & Finch poster girl win. Maybe *Daddy* will give Tyler a good tip and help us out even more."

Tyler leapt off the auction block and walked over to Jessica, who threw her arms around him—her eyes on Becca. Tyler smiled awkwardly at the girls.

"Man, I wish I had $101 so I could have outbid her." Becca plopped back into her chair.

Jacie leaned against the bake sale table. "Me too."

● ● ●

"I still can't believe that *you* are going to tutor a child." Becca threw her head back and laughed. "I'm trying to picture it."

Solana groaned. "Good thing my uncle's worth it." She cringed at the mental picture of herself, sitting across a table from a squirmy fifth-grader. "I guess this kid needs to review his math skills once school starts. He better not do anything gross, like pick his nose or breathe with his mouth open." She rested her elbow on the McKinnons' patio table and took another gulp of Coke.

Jacie gave Solana a motherly pat on the cheek. "Just think of Manuel. He'd do it for you."

"Yeah, yeah, yeah."

Becca crunched an ice cube. "Would you rather tutor or baby-sit? Kara, Kassy, Tyra, Hannah, and I are going to baby-sit."

"No way!"

Solana looked again at the envelope in the middle of the table. Jacie, Tyler, and Kara had brought in $340 alone. She'd lost count after Becca's turn on the block. She clutched her hands together, resisting the urge to grab the envelope and count the money.

"No, Solana," Jacie warned, reading Solana's thoughts. "We can't count the money until all the fund-raisers are finished next week. We agreed."

"It'll be more fun that way." Hannah snatched the envelope and laid it on her lap. "There—I've removed the temptation."

Solana smacked the table. "Aren't you curious at all?"

"Of course," Tyler said. "But unlike you, we have self-control."

Solana stuck her tongue out at Tyler. "I just want to know if we have enough to make a difference."

Becca refilled her Coke. "Are you kidding? The money for Jacie alone will help pay for something."

"We should have just let people take turns buying her all afternoon."

Tyler nudged Jacie. "We would have made enough to pay off Manuel's ranch."

Jacie's cheeks flushed. "Let's not go that far."

Solana shook her finger at Jacie. "Don't put down your talent, girl. If we don't make enough money, my next plan is to auction off your paintings."

"Maybe we can sell one or two at the garage sale," Hannah suggested. "I'm sure people would take those over secondhand clothes and old baby furniture any day."

Jacie looked at Solana for approval.

"Hey," Solana said. "I'm the one who suggested it."

"Okay," Jacie nodded. "I'll paint something special tomorrow—maybe a picture of the ranch, or your uncle's horses."

"And I'm sure my mom has an old frame around here somewhere," Becca said. "We'll make it look really professional."

"Don't forget to sign it," Tyler insisted.

Jacie rolled her eyes.

"She *always* signs her paintings, you idiot," Becca said.

"I'm just making sure," Tyler said.

Solana traced the rim of her glass with her finger and smiled. With her friends in charge, Manuel didn't need to worry about losing anything.

chapter 5

Solana sat cross-legged on the floor of Jacie's artist shack. She stuffed the money from the garage sale into the manila envelope, along with the proceeds from the servant auction and three bake sales.

"Even my parents were shocked by how well the garage sale went." Hannah knelt between Becca and Jacie. "We tried to have one before moving to Copper Ridge and it was a big waste of time. The twins made more on their lemonade stand than we did. Dad said, 'Never again.'"

"I'm glad he changed his mind for us." Solana squeezed the envelope, remembering the flocks of people who'd shown up in Hannah's front yard that morning. Jacie's painting of Manuel's horses and a sketch of Dragonfly Pond sold in the first half-hour. The money called to her from inside the envelope, begging to be counted. She implored Becca with her eyes. "Please say it's time."

"Oh, okay."

"Yes!" Solana pinched the metal tabs on the envelope.

"Wait." Hannah reached into her skirt pocket and pulled out a small envelope. "Here's something to add to it. My youth group took a love offering. So did the people from my parents' Bible study."

Solana stared at the envelope that Hannah held out to her. Hannah had raised extra money on her own—for her?

"I told them your uncle's story," Hannah explained, "and you wouldn't believe the response."

"Do they know that I'm not a—you know? Because when they find out, they might want their money back."

"They know." Hannah smiled. "It made them want to show the love of Christ even more."

Solana took the envelope from Hannah, looking into her gentle blue eyes. It hit her that even if those people at Hannah's church didn't know about her not being a Christian, Hannah did—and she still took the collection. It felt like a soft finger touched her heart. She felt warmed and cared for. She returned Hannah's smile. "Thanks so much."

"If I can help in any other way, let me know."

"I set out a collection can in the office at the community center." Becca reached behind Jacie's easel and pulled out a can marked SAVE THE DRAGONFLY RANCH. She opened it and dumped the contents into Solana's envelope.

"And I left one in Raggs By Razz." Jacie jumped up and grabbed a can off her small table. On hers she'd sketched a picture of Manuel's ranch house. She handed the can to Solana. "Keep the can as a memento."

"Wow, thanks." Solana emptied the change and stacked the bills on Jacie's desk. "I don't believe this. I never expected you guys to earn extra money on your own."

"Man, I feel like a jerk and a half." Tyler slapped his leg. "I didn't think to leave a can anywhere."

"Yeah," Becca teased. "You could have at least stood on the corner with your guitar and let people throw pennies into the case."

Tyler started to get up. "I still could."

Jacie grabbed his arm. "That's okay, Tyler. You put in extra time at the Abbotts and made $50 more than you thought you would. That more than makes up for it."

"Aw, Ty." Becca frowned. "It must have been so awful for you—stuck at the home of your beautiful former girlfriend, fishing leaves out of her swimming pool while she brought you chilled glasses of lemonade."

"Yeah, it was pretty rough." Tyler leaned back. He rubbed his eye. "One of those tiny umbrellas Jessica stuck in the lemonade glass poked me in the eye." He sighed. "But it was for a good cause."

"Well, thanks for the sacrifice." Solana looked into the bulging envelope again. When she and her friends had talked about fund-raising, she'd never imagined making so much money. Surely it would be enough to help with Manuel's medical bills, or a payment on the ranch loan.

"Let's count it." Becca reached for the envelope.

Solana pushed the stack of bills toward Becca. She stuck her hand inside the envelope and handed some money to Jacie, Tyler, and Hannah. She spilled the rest on the floor in front of her.

For the next few minutes the only sounds in Jacie's shack were the flutter of bills, the clink of change, and the whispers of Becca and Jacie counting under their breath. Solana's heart pounded with excitement. Her stack included a hundred-dollar bill and two fifties, in addition to the many fives, tens, and ones.

"I have $286 here." Solana took a sketchpad and a charcoal pencil from the desk and wrote down her amount.

Her friends wrote their amounts down as she counted the remaining change. When Solana totaled everything they had raised, she gasped. "Is this for real?" She added the numbers again, then a third time.

Tyler looked over her shoulder. "Manuel can probably make *two* ranch payments with that."

"This is awesome!" Becca punched the air. "I knew it."

Jacie and Hannah both clasped her hands and looked at the ceiling at the same time. "Thank You, thank You, thank You." They looked at each other and laughed.

"Oh *puh-leaz!*" Solana jumped up. "Come on. Let's take the money to my uncle now." She threw open the shack door. "He'll be so happy."

● ● ●

"His room is this way—406." Solana pointed toward a hallway marked Rooms 400–415. She wanted to break into a sprint. Her feet simply couldn't move fast enough. Manuel would be so excited, so grateful. Solana tried to predict the scene in her mind—Manuel's face full of gratitude as he accepted the money and thanked them all for saving his ranch.

When they reached Manuel's room, Solana knocked lightly on the door before poking her head in. "*Buenas tardes*—I brought friends with me." Solana led the group in.

She sat on the edge of Manuel's bed and leaned over to hug him. Manuel turned his head. "*Hola*. Nice to see you all."

"Hi, Mr. Luz." Becca waved from the foot of Manuel's bed.

Manuel pushed the button to raise his bed up a little higher. He chuckled. "Manuel, not Mr. Luz. You have been helping out at the ranch so much—you are like *familia* now."

"How are you feeling?" Hannah asked. Solana expected her to stand back, uncomfortable about the idea of being in a man's hospital room. Instead she chose the chair beside Manuel's bed.

"You look good," Jacie said.

Solana took a close look at him. He looked stronger every time she saw him, but still tired, and—there was something else in his eyes. What was it?

Manuel ran his hand over his cheeks and chin. "Not bad for a guy who needs to shave, huh?" He pushed back his dinner tray. "So, what are you all doing here on a Saturday? You should be out swimming or—"

Tyler cut him off. "Or working at the ranch?"

Manuel laughed. "No, you have been there enough. Maricella and Ramón say you are there almost every day. How do have time for anything else?"

Becca almost bounced out of her chair. "We have found time for other things. We—"

"Hey, let me tell him." Solana grinned at her uncle, who looked puzzled.

Manuel studied the group. "What are you up to?"

"*Tio* Manuel." Solana took a deep breath. "Mamá and Papá told me that you could lose the ranch because of the accident."

Manuel opened his mouth but Solana kept talking. "I know you probably didn't want anyone to know, but I'm glad that I found out. It gave me and my friends a chance to help you."

She held out the envelope. At first Manuel only stared at it. Then he reached for it, his hand trembling.

"We raised money to help with your bills, so you won't lose the ranch." Solana tucked a strand of dark hair behind her ear.

Hannah leaned forward. "There are so many people praying for you, Mr. Luz—I mean Manuel. Everyone who heard your story was excited to contribute."

Manuel held the envelope, staring at it like he didn't know what to do with it. Solana sat on the bed. "Open it. We didn't just empty our piggy banks—we raised a lot."

Tears filled Manuel's eyes. Solana was taken back. The only time she'd ever seen any men in her family cry was at funerals. He must be so relieved, she thought. He could concentrate on getting well instead of worrying about his debts.

Manuel's hands trembled a little as he pinched the clasps and opened the envelope. He reached inside and pulled out a handful of bills, sucking in his breath when he saw the money. "How did you get all this?"

Solana couldn't talk fast enough, as she recapped all the ways that she and her friends had come up with to earn money. The only thing she didn't mention was her camp money. Manuel would refuse that contribution if he knew about it.

"You worked so hard." Manuel wiped his eyes and took a deep breath. "I do not know how to thank you."

Hannah reached for a tissue and handed it to Manuel.

Solana took hold of his hand. "It's okay. We loved doing it." She tried to look into his eyes but he avoided her gaze. "Uncle Manuel, what's wrong?"

"You do not understand." Despite his efforts, Manuel's tears kept coming.

"Maybe we should have called first," Becca whispered to Jacie.

"I feel bad," Jacie whispered back. "Having us all here is probably too much."

Manuel shook his head. "No. I owe more than you realize. And the longer I stay in this hospital the more I owe to doctors." He laid his hand on the envelope in his lap. "It could never be . . ."

Solana lowered her head. She could barely get out the words that she knew were about to come out of Manuel's mouth—words that she'd rather say herself than hear from him. "It's not enough."

c h a p t e r 6

Solana ran the metal comb through Shadow's coarse brown mane. She laid the comb down and stroked the horse's neck. What would happen to Shadow if Manuel lost the ranch? The idea of somebody else grooming her favorite horse fell on her heart like a lead weight.

What else could she and her friends do? Maricella had the envelope of money, from which she would pay as many bills as possible. But how long would the money last?

Ramón's voice startled her. "I am having some serious déjà vu right now."

Solana turned around. She set Shadow's comb on the stool beside her and wiped her hands on her jeans. Her mind went back to that afternoon in March when Cameron Morelli wrecked her science fair project and she'd escaped to the ranch. That meeting with Ramón had done more than save her project. It had sparked her first real love—a love that went too far too fast.

Everything in her wanted to run to Ramón. She knew that if she did, Ramón would never push her away. He'd hold her while she cried. He'd assure her that everything would work out somehow. But she held back, closing her eyes against the present and the past. *I can't take the risk of being close to him.*

"You okay?" Ramón asked, his tender voice melting her heart.

Solana opened her eyes. She nodded, afraid to speak.

"Liar." Ramón took a step toward Solana. "You're not very good at hiding your feelings you know."

After all they'd shared, how could she expect to hide her sadness from him? "Yeah. Especially around you." Desperate to change the subject to something that wouldn't make her cry, she said, "Hey, thanks for all the extra help lately. We can really use it now that all the relatives have gone home. Do you really have time, though, with your summer classes?"

"Oh, sure." Ramón leaned against the stall. "My mom is taking real estate classes on top of her full-time job, so she's rarely home. The empty condo is too quiet. I'd rather be here."

"But Maricella says you offered to work without pay. Can you afford that?"

"For a while." Ramón made tiny circles on the floor of the stable with the toe of his boot. "You know your aunt and uncle won't let me work completely for free. Maricella sent me home with a pile of homemade tortillas yesterday. Then she tried to pay me a little this morning, out of that stash that you and your friends gave her."

"Why wouldn't you take it?"

"Because I know she needs it for other things." Ramón smiled at Solana. "That was great what you guys did, by the way. I wish I could have helped."

Solana kicked at some loose straw. "A lot of good it did."

"It *did* do some good. Do you know how relieved Maricella is to have that money?"

"They'll still eventually lose their home."

"Not as quickly. You've given them a little longer to find a solution." Ramón touched Solana's arm. Electricity ran from that spot to the top of her head. How long had it been since Ramón touched her? Not since they'd broken up—unless she counted the few times when they brushed arms accidentally, or bumped into each other while working. For an awkward moment they stood, just looking at each other.

Ramón finally broke the silence. "Hey, guess what?" He dug into the pocket of his jeans and pulled out a folded sheet of paper. "I have some good news."

"Great. I can use some good news."

Ramón handed her the paper. Before she had a chance to read it he told her, "MIT accepted me. The letter came today."

"Really?" Solana forced a stiff smile. "But I thought you had another year at Copper Ridge."

"Since I was running out of prerequisite classes, one of my instructors talked me into applying for next semester. He even handed me a stack of scholarship applications so I'd have no excuse. He wrote me an excellent recommendation."

Solana stared at the MIT letterhead. It looked so official, so important—and so final. She could almost see the first sentence declaring, "Ramón is leaving Copper Ridge." She forced herself to read the letter, her heart wadded up somewhere at the bottom of her stomach. She folded the letter and handed it back to him.

"You got a *full* scholarship? That's amazing." Every syllable hurt her throat. *Why don't I feel happier for him?*

The boyish crooked smile that she'd fallen in love with spread across his lips. "Yeah, I was pretty surprised. Unfortunately I didn't make the deadline for fall. I don't start until after winter break."

"Good." The word popped out before Solana could catch herself. "I mean, that'll give you more time to prepare for the big move," she said, confused by her own feelings. "Congratulations." She forced another smile. "You totally deserve it."

"You were the first person I wanted to tell—well, besides my mom."

Solana stepped back. "I was?"

"Well, yeah. Who else would appreciate getting into a college like MIT?"

"Especially after only a year of community college." Solana opened her arms and drew Ramón into a congratulatory hug. She pulled back before she had a chance to really feel the warmth of his embrace. "I'm so happy for you."

Ramón refolded the paper and stuffed it back into his pocket. "Thanks. I'm really excited."

Shadow nuzzled the back of Solana's head. She reached around and stroked him. "Um. Since I was getting ready to take Shadow for a ride . . ." She almost let the question "Do you want to join me?" spill out. *Why would I ask a thing like that? One touch on the arm and I'm melting again? Wake up!*

Ramón grinned. "I figured you were going for a ride. But let me guess—you need to go by yourself, so you can think."

"Ah, you know me too well." She patted Shadow's neck. "I'll be back to help you soon."

As Ramón walked outside, Solana pressed her face into Shadow's mane, willing herself to hold together. To stay strong. To stuff her feelings into a safe place.

● ● ●

A warm breeze blew through Solana's long, dark hair. She perched on Shadow's back, holding him still so she could watch the *tesoros puros* grazing in the distance. Pretty soon she'd have to say good-bye to them, too. Her lip quivered. She wanted to cry out, "I'm losing everything—first Ramón, and now the ranch, the horses, and even the *tesoros puros*."

But who would hear her cry?

"God will listen, if you call on Him," Hannah had said a bajillion times before. And her friends would agree. But would He? Had He listened to the prayers of her friends, or the kids in Hannah's youth group? It didn't seem like it. It felt more like He'd teased her and all her *Brio* friends—letting them make just enough money to hope for the best, but not enough to solve the real problem.

She saw the tree where she and Ramón had made the decision that changed their relationship forever. A tear trickled down her cheek. She didn't bother to brush it away.

Breaking up was the right thing to do, she recited to herself, as she had almost daily since she and Ramón decided to give each other space. But she'd learned since then they could never be friends either. How could two people get as close as they had and go back to being "just friends"? They'd always want more. Every time she saw him, she wanted more.

Maybe it will be easier when Ramón is gone.

It sure didn't feel like it.

● ● ●

"Why do I care if Ramón leaves?" Solana clenched her fists in frustration. "I should be relieved. I won't have to worry about running into him all the time. Or how to act around him." *Or be tempted to tell him the honest truth—that I still love him and want to get back together.*

Solana's friends sat around her on a stack of hay bales behind Manuel's stable.

"It's just harder because you're losing two things at the same time," Becca said. "Ramón is part of the ranch."

"It's too much change at once," Jacie said.

"Sometimes change turns out to be a good thing," Hannah chimed in. Everyone stared at her. Solana wanted to yell at her—to tell her what she could do with her stupid pat answers. They always seemed to fly out when Solana wanted to hear them the least.

"Before you get mad, hear me out." Hannah leaned forward. "When I moved here from Michigan, it meant leaving all my friends, my home-school group—everything. Then my parents made the decision to send me to public high school—another big change. No offense, but I expected to hate it."

"Really, Hannah?" Becca looked at Jacie, Tyler, and Solana individually, her mouth hanging open in faux disbelief. "You never made that clear."

Tyler turned to Becca and whispered, "She didn't like Stony Brook at first? All this time I thought she loved us. I'm hurt." He stabbed his fist to his chest.

"That's exactly my point," Hannah said. "Look what has happened since then. I have a great group of friends, I'm on the newspaper staff at school—I could go on and on. God used those big changes in my life for good."

"That's true," Becca said, getting serious again. "And look what happened with Alvaro. I didn't want him as a permanent member of my family. Now I can't imagine life without him."

Jacie and Tyler nodded, as if the stories sparked personal memories of change-turned-good for them, too. Then Jacie took another look at Solana and her face filled with compassion. "Of course having something taken from you is much different than moving or gaining a little brother. Loss hurts far more."

Solana rested her elbows on her knees. She gazed out over Manuel's fields, which seemed to stretch on forever. One of his horses whinnied from his corral. "You have no idea how much."

Jacie offered a reassuring smile. "But we aren't going anywhere. We'll help you through it."

"Maybe Ramón needs to leave in order for you to really let go of him," Hannah suggested. "You'll be able to concentrate on something else besides wondering how to act around him."

"Like what?" Solana asked. "The ranch will be gone too."

Jacie straightened up. "You know what you need?"

"About two hundred thousand dollars?" Solana stared listlessly at Jacie's hopeful face.

"No." Jacie shook her head. "You need something to remember this place—something really special."

Solana shrugged. "Like what?"

Jacie twirled one of her ringlets, thinking. "How about an album of pictures? I'll help you put it together. We can get some fancy scrapbook materials at a craft store and everything."

"I'm sure my mom will let you have some snapshots from Alvaro's birthday party," Becca said. "There's some great ones of Manuel and Ramón helping the kids ride Carmen."

"And I'll take some new ones over the next few weeks," Hannah promised.

Solana stood. Would pictures really be enough, once the ranch was gone? She had hundreds of them—of family parties, her with her cousins riding and playing by Dragonfly Pond. For the past two nights she'd looked through old photo albums and ended up in tears. As usual her friends were trying to help. She couldn't tell them, "No, your idea isn't special enough."

Instead, Solana said, "That might be fun, Jace. I'll think about it." She twisted to work out a kink in her back. "We should get back to work."

For the rest of the afternoon her mind was flooded with possibilities of how she could remember the ranch. A time capsule? No.

It would have to be something that she could look at anytime—something permanent.

Something permanent? She stopped in her tracks. *I have the perfect idea.*

chapter 7

Rock music blared through the sound system in BodyArt By Design. Solana tried to ignore her mother hovering behind her at the counter.

Mamá peered into the glass case that displayed tattoo guns, piercing tools, and a variety of body jewelry. She looked at Solana as if she'd just volunteered for torture.

"Take your time looking through the book," a tall, muscular man told Solana. He had a pierced eyebrow, and tattoos completely decorated his arms.

Solana got a closer look at one of his tattoos as the man dropped a catalog in front of her. *Now there's a walking example of why some people find tattoos offensive.*

He took a quick swig of a Sprite and covered a burp with his fist before walking behind a partition to help his next customer. "Be with you soon," he called over his shoulder.

Mamá cringed when she heard the distant buzz of the tattooing gun. "Are you sure that you want to do this, Solana?" she whispered.

Solana forced herself not to roll her eyes. Couldn't Mamá at least *try* to hide her feelings? "Yes, Mamá, I'm sure." She envied Pilar for waiting until she was old enough to get a tattoo without Mamá's signature approval. She probably wanted to avoid a scene like this. Solana tried to concentrate on the catalog. She smiled when she saw a whole page marked "horses." But when she studied each horse in detail, her shoulders slumped in despair.

"That one looks nice." Mamá pointed to a black leaping horse.

Solana shook her head. "No. Look how chunky the legs are." She let out a heavy sigh. "They all look like cartoon horses. I want one that reminds me of Shadow." She flipped the pages halfheartedly. Maybe she should forget the whole thing. All summer she'd been secretly stashing what little extra cash she had to get a tattoo. She could always give it to Maricella instead. *But I want to do this.* Solana turned another disappointing page.

"Come, *mi'ja*." Mamá put her hand on Solana's arm. "We can try another day—this weekend maybe. There's probably a better place in Denver."

Solana flipped one more page. She was about to slam the book closed when a picture jumped out at her. "No, wait. I found it." She pointed to the picture.

Mamá looked more closely. "*That?*"

"Yes." Solana smiled, feeling a surge of satisfaction shoot up her spine. "It's perfect."

● ● ●

Solana carefully pulled back the cellophane covering her tattoo to show Pilar. "What do you think?"

"It's hard to tell under the icky-looking scab." Pilar smiled. "But

I'm proud of you, girl! It'll look great when it's healed."

Solana rubbed her arm. "I didn't expect it to hurt so much."

"Wait 'til tomorrow, when it feels like someone scoured your shoulder with sandpaper."

Solana winced.

"But it's worth it." Pilar moved closer to Solana and examined the tattoo in more detail. "Why did you pick that design?"

"You don't like it?"

"No, I do. I'm just curious why you picked it."

Solana replaced the covering. "It's to remember the ranch."

"Oh, I get it." Pilar winked. "I bet the guys will think it's sexy. My new boyfriend loves mine."

Solana settled back against a pile of pillows. She pictured herself showing the tattoo to Ramón. What would he think of it? She pushed the idea out of her mind. "I didn't get it for a guy—I got it for myself."

Pilar flopped back on the bed. "You mean you didn't get it for *Ramón?*"

"No!"

"I don't care what you say, Solana. You still love him. I can tell when I see you together at the ranch." She propped herself up on her elbow.

"Yeah, well, no matter how I feel, he's leaving in a few months. Plus, even if he were staying, we can't be together. Don't make me list the reasons why again, please."

"Okay. I'll never understand your reasons, but okay." Pilar looked up at Solana. "Have you dated anyone seriously since Ramón?"

Solana snorted, thinking back to her last few dates—the guy she'd been with at the movies, the night that Tyler's sister got caught seeing *The River Runs Downhill*—what a baby he'd been. Ramón never would have acted so immature. Then there was Todd, who'd only wanted to make out. He not only got mad when she said she wasn't into making out with guys she hardly knew, but he laughed when she explained that she was trying to take relationships slowly and seriously.

Nothing had changed since she dated Ramón. Just like before, none of the guys were interested in talking about science, or the stars, or anything else that required any brains. "All the guys seem like idiots compared to Ramón."

Pilar sighed. "See what happens when you find the perfect guy? It ruins your dating life forever."

Solana punched a pillow. "Oh great! So there's no hope." Once again she felt swept away by her own thoughts—thoughts that Pilar would never understand. Why couldn't she go back to being the same old boy-crazy Solana? Why wasn't it fun to flirt with every guy she saw and dress in ways that she knew attracted them? Had Ramón really had that much of an effect on her, or had she changed? Oh, what was the difference? She had more important things to worry about now.

"Pilar, can you think of any ideas for helping Manuel keep his ranch?" Solana watched the ceiling fan spin. "There must be something we can do."

Pilar shook her head. "What Manuel needs is money, and nobody has any." She looked at Solana. "Solana, it isn't your job to save Manuel's ranch—you're a kid."

Solana rolled her eyes.

Pilar sat up. "Come on. You've already helped more than anyone else in the family has. You make me look like a slacker—I was only able to come out for a week." She scowled. "And then there's Elijo—Mr. Helpful."

Solana scowled too at the mention of her brother. "I can't believe he hasn't been out to help at all. He could. He doesn't even have a job."

"Oh, but he has a girlfriend," Pilar said.

"My friends have lots of other responsibilities and they find time to help me at the ranch almost every day. Elijo should learn from their example."

"Yeah, well, your friends are unique."

"That's for sure."

Pilar wrapped her arm around Solana. "So why not thank them for their help by having some fun with them before school starts? Instead of knocking yourself out at the ranch every waking moment, go riding while you still can."

"That does sound nice." Solana leaned into her sister's embrace. Maybe it was time to give up and move on.

● ● ●

"Left, Hannah, left," Becca shouted. "Tug on the other side of the reins."

"I'm trying." Hannah untangled the reins from around her hands. "This horse only wants to go right."

Despite her sadness, Solana couldn't help laughing. All morning Hannah had provided the group with comic relief that only a completely inexperienced rider could do.

Solana turned to Becca, who was cracking up. "We'll be lucky to get back to the ranch with Hannah and Carmen both in one piece."

Becca glanced back at Hannah, who had barely avoided riding Carmen into a ditch. "At least she's facing the right end of the horse now."

An instant replay image of Hannah mounting Carmen, only to end up facing the horse's rear, carried Solana again to a full laugh. "We should have kept her like that."

Becca laughed harder. "You're mean."

"I heard that, Solana," Hannah called from the back of the line.

"That was my intention!"

"Oh, ignore those two." Jacie slowed her horse down and allowed Hannah to catch up. "You're doing fine."

"Before you know it, you'll be ready for the Kentucky Derby." Tyler leaned forward, hunching his body into jockey position. "And it's Thunderbolt on the outside. He's a shoo-in to win, folks. No! Carmen wins by a nose! What an upset!"

Solana searched the surrounding pastureland for her herd of mustangs. An excruciating sorrow gripped her like a vice. She wanted to memorize everything around her—each tree, the way the mountains towered over her uncle's pasture like a protective wall, the smell of evergreens mixed with sun-dried grass and soil. She closed her eyes and breathed in deeply. Her shoulder still burned slightly but she resisted rubbing the raw tattooed area.

"Uh, Solana?" Becca looked around. "Where are we going?"

Solana shrugged. If it were up to her, she would just ride without stopping. But her friends, especially Becca, probably wouldn't enjoy it much. "Hannah hasn't seen Dragonfly Pond up close yet. We can go there."

"Oh," Jacie sighed. "I love Dragonfly Pond. It's so pretty."

They rode the rest of the way in silence, almost unheard of for the group. The closer they got to the pond the harder Solana fought against the threat of tears. How could a tattoo ever be enough to commemorate this place? It seemed like a perfect tribute two days ago. Now the idea felt ridiculous. Not that she regretted getting it. She liked the way it looked. But it didn't lessen her pain over losing the ranch. Nothing could take the place of spending days there and riding the breathtaking trails surrounding Manuel's property.

"Why do you call it Dragonfly Pond?" Hannah's voice sounded far off, as though in a dream. Solana knew the question was directed at her, but her mouth refused to open in an answer. She dismounted

Shadow at the pond and let Becca explain about the dragonflies.

Tyler tied his horse to a tree and strolled over to Hannah, who still sat helplessly on Carmen. "Allow me, m'lady." Tyler led Carmen to the nearest tree and tied her before holding his hand out to Hannah.

"Thank you, kind sir." She reached for Tyler's hand. Solana stood back and watched Hannah try to slide gracefully off Carmen, by swinging her right leg in front, barely missing the horse's head.

"No, no!" Solana cringed. "Swing your leg around back."

"Sorry." Hannah obeyed, doing surprisingly well, until her foot touched the ground and her left foot caught in the stirrup. She hopped up and down on her right foot as she tried to free the other. Tyler stepped in front of her just as she tugged her foot free and lost her balance. She fell against Tyler, knocking both of them to the ground.

Becca covered her face, screaming with laughter along with Jacie.

"Are you guys okay?" Jacie doubled over, barely able to speak.

Solana shook her head and smirked as Hannah scrambled to her feet.

"Tyler, I'm so sorry." Hannah brushed off her baggy shorts and held her hand out to Tyler. "Here, let me help you."

Tyler waved Hannah's hand away and sat up, his face flushed with embarrassment. "Gee, Hannah, if I'd known you liked me so much . . ."

Hannah turned at least three shades of red as Tyler joined the explosion of laughter. Hannah's lips moved in an attempt to say something, but she couldn't seem to find any words. She covered her face, trying to regain her composure.

"Well," she looked up and smiled sheepishly. "I guess I need to work on my dismount."

That only made the group laugh more.

Solana raised her eyebrows. "Yeah, you could say that." She grinned as Hannah laughed at her own statement. "Thanks, Hannah. Every time I've felt sad today, you've made me laugh."

"Glad I could brighten your day."

Tyler hopped up and whacked dirt off of his clothes and body. "Okay, I confess. I put Hannah up to all this. She's an expert horsewoman but I told her to act clueless. Thought you could use the cheering up, Sol—worked, huh?" He smacked Solana's shoulder.

"Ow!" Solana grabbed her shoulder and smacked Tyler back. Once again she felt the tattoo gun sending a thousand pricks into her skin.

"What?" Tyler took a step back.

Solana opened her mouth to tell Tyler and the rest about her tattoo but quickly changed her mind. They'd probably give her a hard time, saying that remembering Manuel's ranch was only an excuse to get what she wanted. *Getting a tattoo was my choice and I don't feel like justifying my choices today.*

"Sorry, Ty." She patted Tyler on the shoulder that she'd smacked. "My shoulder is sore. I must have gotten sunburned."

"Must be some sunburn."

"You need stronger sunscreen." Becca ran over to join Solana and Tyler. She started to lift Solana's sleeve but Solana jerked her shoulder back.

Jacie sat on the grass and crossed her legs. "We *have* been out in the sun a lot, between helping at the ranch and doing the fundraisers." She gasped suddenly. "Oh look, a little frog." They got up slowly and tiptoed to the edge of the pond.

Solana walked over and joined her at the bank. She knelt and examined the frog that Jacie was studying, like a perfect subject for her next painting.

"That's not a frog, Jace—it's a toad. You can tell by his dry, warty skin." She took a closer look. "It looks like a boreal toad. But

I doubt it. Boreals are endangered in Colorado." She stood up and put her hands on her hips. "It better not be a boreal toad. I'd be so mad if we had an endangered species right here at the ranch and couldn't stick around to enjoy it."

Jacie reached out to stroke the toad, but he hopped out of reach. She snapped her fingers in defeat. She sat back on her heels, staring thoughtfully over the pond. "I wish I had my sketchbook. I want to paint a picture of this pond for your uncle." She turned to Solana. "Do you think he'd like that?"

"He'd love it." Solana lowered her face, once again fighting back sadness.

"This whole ranch is gorgeous," Becca said breathlessly. "It reminds me of a farm I went to when I was little. Every year it was turned into a pumpkin patch, with scarecrows and a big hay maze." Becca walked over to the edge of the pond and picked up a stick. She poked at the water, watching a trio of dragonflies dance across the surface. She screwed up her face in disgust. "Eew!" Becca pointed to a bunch of reeds growing out of the water. "What is *that?*"

Tyler hopped up on a fallen tree trunk and ran across it. "What?"

Solana followed Tyler. She squatted on the tree trunk to get closer to the reeds that Becca pointed to. At first she only saw what looked like fluttering wings. She looked more closely and recognized a young dragonfly clinging to the top of a stem. "Hey, you guys." She motioned to Hannah and Jacie. "Come here and look at this."

Everyone gathered around, watching in quiet awe. "What is it?" Jacie asked softly.

Solana smiled. "A dragonfly."

Hannah scrunched her nose. "But it's so ugly."

"It is now, but wait until it's finished."

Jacie sucked in her breath. "Is he shedding his skin?"

"Yes." The dragonfly's wings flapped wildly in his struggle to break free from the confines of the old skin. Time seemed to stop as he shed his final layer and hovered among the reeds. "It has taken him a long time to change from a nymph to what he is now," Solana explained, unable to take her eyes off of the freshly emerged creature. "Nymphs are born underwater and stay there for two years."

"That *is* a long time to hold your breath," Tyler said.

Solana kept her attention on the dragonfly. "The nymph sheds his skin 15 times before climbing up a plant or a blade of grass. Then voilà! We have a dragonfly."

"Aren't there like 500 types of dragonflies?" Tyler asked.

Solana sat back, her eyes still on the reed that the larva had used as his home for so long. "More like 5,000."

"Wow," Jacie breathed. "Isn't God amazing?"

"Yes," Hannah and Tyler said.

Solana picked up a small rock and tossed it into the pond. *If He's so amazing, why is He letting me lose something I love so much?*

"Hey." Becca jumped up, breaking everyone out of the moment of wonder. "We can't stop trying to save this place."

"There's nothing else we can do, Becca." Solana picked up another rock, wanting to throw it hard enough to shatter something.

Becca hopped down from the log. "How do you know? Just because the fund-raisers didn't bring in enough—maybe we can try something else." Solana didn't even try to think of a new plan. If there were something else, wouldn't she have thought of it by now?

"It's not like you to give up, Solana," Becca persisted.

"I haven't given up—I've just accepted reality." *A reality that's tearing my heart out.*

"Do you have a brilliant new idea, Becca?" Tyler's voice mirrored Solana's frustration.

Becca stared at the ground. "Well, no. But if we all think some more, maybe one of us will come up with something."

Hannah sat beside Jacie. "Maybe God wants us to pray harder."

"I don't know how hard God expects you guys to pray." Solana stood up and studied the beauty around her. She really didn't want to give up. It had just seemed to make sense. "But I'm willing to think some more."

chapter 8

Solana looked at her clock again—1:16 A.M.—and she hadn't gotten a bit of sleep. How could she have even considered giving up on her family? Familia *is the only thing that lasts*. Her parents had instilled that in her since birth. But what more could she do? She flipped onto her back. *What good is insomnia if I can't use it to come up with something brilliant?*

The full moon shone through her window onto the mural of wild mustangs she and Jacie had painted the summer before. Alessandro, the unicorn foal in the painting, ran ahead of the herd. Solana closed her eyes and tried to lull herself to sleep by playing out the scene from the mural in her mind. Alessandro led the mustangs through the pasture and into a breathtaking grove of aspen and Rocky Mountain maples. Then suddenly the mustangs were drinking from Dragonfly Pond, and once again Solana was wide awake.

She sat up and turned on her bedside light.

Maybe I could listen to music.

No, that would wake up everyone else in the house.

She punched her mattress. She groaned and got out of bed, stretching her sleep-deprived arms, searching her room for something to either pass the night or put her to sleep.

In the dim light she spotted a pile of magazines in the corner by her desk. The pile had been accumulating since May when she'd started receiving the three free magazine subscriptions she'd won. She'd been ignoring the magazines because they brought back the disappointment and feelings of failure that she'd only won fourth place at the district science fair.

She stuck her tongue out at the small mountain, then sighed. "Oh, I might as well read the stupid things. Maybe they'll put me to sleep." She grabbed the top two issues and flopped onto her bed. *Astronomy Journal* only reminded her that she was missing camp, so she tossed it aside for *The Great Outdoors*.

To give herself some dumb sense of adventure, she opened the glossy cover to the contents, closed her eyes, and jabbed her finger onto the page. She flipped to the article she'd chosen and was immediately swept away. An hour later she had finished the entire magazine. She rested her head on the pillow, but the articles swam through her mind. Sighing, she got up and grabbed another magazine off the pile. She decided to read it cover to cover, minus the "close your eyes and pick" game. But a title jumped out at her.

"Preserving the Planet, One Endangered Species at a Time."

Now here was a subject she couldn't get enough of. She flipped to the starting page and dove into it. The article drew her in, using a series of true short stories, of ordinary people who had discovered endangered species in their area and worked to protect them. In the process they had saved land that might have otherwise been devastated by office buildings or shopping centers.

Her heart thumped with excitement. She sprang from her bed and grabbed a pair of sweats from a pile on the floor.

She padded downstairs in stockinged feet and headed for the den. She dropped her pile of magazines next to the computer and sat in the swivel chair. After switching the computer on she drummed her fingers on the mouse pad, waiting for the machine to boot up and dial her Internet connection. In case one of her friends also happened to be up at this insane hour, she got her IM up and running. Typing in the URL for the Preserve the Planet Web site, she felt her stomach waking up. Hadn't Mamá put some leftover enchiladas in the refrigerator?

"Later," she told her stomach.

Her jaw dropped when the Web site opened. "This is incredible." Species after species appeared on the screen with each click of the mouse—rare mammals, insects, birds, and small rodents peeking out of hiding places.

"Wait! What was that one?"

She clicked on the "Back" button.

"No, that's not it," she muttered to herself. She clicked "Back" one more time.

"There," she said to no one. "The boreal toad."

She admired the small warty creature. Then her heart stopped. "Yes! This is it!"

● ● ●

Becca yawned into the phone. "Hello?"

"Get out of bed, Sleeping Beauty. I need your help." Solana took a gulp of strong, heavily sugared coffee.

Becca moaned. "Solana, it's not even six in the morning."

"Hey, I could have called you at two."

"What's going on?"

The floor in the hallway creaked under Papá's heavy footsteps.

Solana got up from the couch and took the phone to her room, waving to Papá in the hall.

"I think I found a way to save Manuel's ranch." Her body buzzed with the dizzying combination of fatigue, caffeine, and excitement.

She told Becca what she discovered during her sleepless night. "I've read about protecting wetlands, open-space initiatives, boreal toads, and agricultural land. The irritating thing is that no one tells how to begin, only that it's important and has been done before." The sound of running water and brushing from Becca's end of the line stopped Solana mid-thought. "Are you brushing your teeth?"

Becca spit. "I need to wake up somehow. At least I'm not going to the bathroom."

"Go for it. I do it all the time when I'm talking to you." Solana lay back on her bed.

"You would." Becca gargled.

"When you finish with your oral hygiene, I need your help."

"Like I know anything about saving the earth. You're the genius."

Solana made her voice sound as tired and helpless as possible. "But the genius's mind is half asleep, and the Internet is a vast wealth of information I simply cannot surf alone. *Please* help me, oh beloved and faithful friend of my youth."

"Give it a rest. I was just kidding. You know I will."

"Okay, call the others and meet me at the library."

"Consider it done." Becca paused. "Can you give us a few hours? I don't think the library opens before dawn."

Solana growled. "Fine. Meet me there at nine."

● ● ●

"Here's a book on preservation." Hannah stuck the thin book between Solana and the computer monitor she was reading. "I found it in the children's section, so it won't be too complicated for us."

Solana took the book and turned glossy pages, filled with photos of forests, lakes, and endangered birds. Then she noticed a picture of a woman naturalist in wire-rimmed glasses and tacky clothes. She checked the copyright date—1971. "Too old." She handed the book back to Hannah. "Thanks for trying."

She puffed up her cheeks and blew the air out slowly. So far the library search had been fruitless.

Jacie pushed her mouse aside. "I keep finding Web sites about groups that protect land and animals, but none of them say how they work."

"Hey, look." Becca pointed to her screen. "Here's something about a group that protects agricultural land. They rely on donations of either money or land."

Solana hopped up. *Agricultural* land. Perfect! "What else does it say?"

She, Jacie, and Hannah hurried over to Becca's computer. Becca read the Web page out loud. But the excitement in her voice dropped, along with Solana's spirits, when she got to the part about the group being located in Kenya.

"This is insane." Solana sank into the chair beside Becca's. "It's like there's a secret underworld for species protection." She lowered her voice. "I can tell you how to have your uncle's farmland preserved, but then I'll have to kill you."

Jacie laughed. She gathered the magazines and books they'd looked through. "We'll come up with something, Solana. Don't worry."

"You didn't find that article last night by accident," Hannah stated with her usual conviction.

"You guys," Tyler shouted from a computer on the other side of the reference section. "Over here—I found something. This is it!"

dragonfly on my shoulder

69

chapter

"Shh!" Jacie and Hannah put their fingers over their lips.

A woman, who sat reading to her little girl on one of the library's plush chairs, looked up and glared at Tyler.

"You're going to get us kicked out, Ty," Becca whispered.

Tyler looked around. "Oh, no. Look! The beehive-hairdo lady with horn-rimmed glasses is coming this way." He grabbed Solana's arm. "Hide me."

Becca and Jacie covered their mouths to hold in laughter but quickly lost the battle, ending up laughing louder than they would have if they hadn't tried to suppress it.

"Do you mind?" A man at a nearby computer scowled at the group. "Some people come to the library to work."

Tyler straightened up and cleared his throat. "Sorry, sir."

Solana smacked the back of Tyler's head. How could he make jokes at a time like this? "Quit goofing around."

"Sorry. Sheesh!"

She hovered over Tyler's shoulder. "What did you find?" Sleep deprivation had left her shaky and irritable. At the same time, the idea of a new possibility filled her with even greater desperation.

Tyler turned obediently back to the screen, with the girls gathered around him. "It says here that endangered species are protected by preserving the land they live on."

"You mean their habitats," Solana offered.

"Yeah, that," Tyler said. "And they do that through groups called conservancies." He pointed to the screen. "This one is called The Greenhouse. They buy land, or people donate it. And you won't believe this—The Greenhouse has an office right here in Copper Ridge."

Solana read the screen—a Web page highlighted with nature photos and slogans about preservation. "Why haven't I ever heard of it?"

Tyler shrugged. "Probably because you never had anything to protect before."

Hannah leaned in closer to read the information. "Where are they located?"

"There's an address at the bottom of the screen." Tyler reached into a basket holding paper scraps and miniature pencils. He handed both to Jacie and pointed to the address. "You write it, Jace—your handwriting is neater than mine."

Jacie wrote quickly in her flowing script.

Solana looked at the address. "I don't recognize the street."

"I do." Becca pushed in her chair. "It's near the community center."

Solana fished her keys out of her jeans pocket. "Let's go. I'll drive."

● ● ●

"Ah yes, one of Copper Ridge's finest neighborhoods." Tyler leaned his elbow halfway out the back window of Solana's parents' car. "It's my big dream to live in that posh apartment complex we just passed." He pointed to a run-down apartment building, in serious need of a paint job.

Hannah clapped her hands together. "Perfect place to raise a family."

"Hey, don't make fun of this neighborhood." Becca pointed to an abandoned brick building. "I took tap lessons right there—back when it was Miss Merriam's School of Dance."

Tyler and Jacie both looked at Becca. Jacie chuckled. "*You* took tap?"

"For one summer when I was eight. My mom wanted me to try an activity that was more feminine than junior basketball league."

Tyler nudged her. "So, when do we get to see photos of you in tights and a frilly little dress with sparkles on the sleeves?"

"Never!" Becca shuddered. "There aren't any, thank goodness!"

Solana ignored her friends and focused on the passing buildings. From the looks of the low-rent neighborhood, with its outdated offices and Mom-and-Pop stores, she understood why she'd never known about The Greenhouse conservancy before today. She glanced back at Jacie. "What number are we looking for again?"

"560B."

Solana squinted to make out the faded block letters on a two-story office stuck between two storefronts. She pointed to it. "There it is."

She'd barely parked before her friends threw their doors open and piled out of the car.

"I hope we didn't need an appointment or something," Hannah said.

Solana slowed down her strides. An appointment? She hadn't even thought of that. The conservancy might not consider helping her if she made a bad first impression by bursting in unannounced.

I'll just have to take my chances, she decided. *I'll act professional, respectful, and like I know what I'm doing. Tio Manuel doesn't have time for me to go home and make appointments.*

"It doesn't look like they're busy," Becca pointed to a small parking lot. "There are only two cars over there."

Solana nodded, trying to shake off her unusual nervousness. *What should I say? I don't want to sound like a dumb kid.* She started planning what she hoped was an intelligent-sounding speech.

"Ladies first." Tyler pulled open the glass door and waved Solana through. The group followed her into the musty-smelling hallway. She looked around for a door marked "560B" or "The Greenhouse."

"It must be upstairs." Becca led the way up a creaky staircase. The green indoor/outdoor carpet was mud-stained and worn in the center of each stair.

Solana bounded ahead of Becca and opened the door marked with the conservancy's name.

The room smelled like the outdoors but was organized and tidy. A fat gray tabby, curled up on the only chair in the room, gave them a bored look.

"Hello," Solana called to the deserted room.

"Be right there," a husky-voiced woman called from an adjoining room.

Hannah and Jacie immediately fell in love with the overstuffed cat. They began smothering him with strokes and coos. Solana walked over to a table set up in the center of the room. Snapshots, samples of rocks, feathers, delicate dried flowers, and other specimens covered the table. In the center sat a detailed diorama. Tyler and Becca joined Solana.

Tyler leaned over the diorama. "I think that's Copper Ridge."

Solana looked more closely. "It is. See?" She pointed to a blue painted surface. "There's Piper Lake."

Becca examined the diorama. "I think that's Misty Falls." She reached out and touched the fake waterfall.

"Don't touch," Solana whispered between her teeth.

"Sorry." Becca put her hand behind her back.

Solana bent to look at the snapshots without picking them up.

"That's a pretty bird." Becca stopped in front of a photo of a colorful bird perched in a fir tree.

"It's a golden-crowned kinglet," Solana explained. "I think that one is a female." Jacie and Hannah wandered over as she pointed out a feather from the many specimens on the table. "That might be a kinglet feather." She told them about other wildlife photos and plants that she recognized—her wonder and excitement building with each one.

"Sorry to keep you waiting," a woman said, startling the group. They all turned to see a tall, sturdy woman with silver-streaked dark hair, wearing baggy jeans and a khaki button-down shirt. The woman smiled and set a thick stack of papers on the desk behind the chair holding the cat. "I'm Ellie Pierson."

Solana stepped forward. "I'd like to speak to the director please."

"I am the director." Ellie held her hand out for Solana to shake. She nodded toward the cat. "And this big lug is Mr. Peabody—Mr. P. for short." A grin lit up her suntanned face, making her friendly, blue-gray eyes sparkle. She picked up Mr. Peabody and sat in his spot on the chair, with him on her lap. "So, what can I do for you?"

Embarrassed by her mistake, Solana took a second to organize her thoughts. She'd expected a conservancy director to look more professional; maybe wearing a lab coat, with a clipboard permanently attached to her hand.

"We saw your Web site," Becca said before Solana got a word

out. "We're looking for someone to help us find out more about land preservation."

"Solana's uncle has a beautiful horse ranch," Jacie said. "But he might lose it."

To Solana's frustration, her friends all tried explaining Manuel's dilemma at once. Ellie looked at Solana inquisitively, then at her friends. She raised her hand to her forehead and narrowed her eyes. A feeling of dread came over Solana, seeing Ellie's perplexed expression. They'd only been talking to this woman for a few minutes and had already managed to tick her off. Why hadn't she told her friends to leave the talking to her?

Ellie waved her hand and smiled. "Okay, time out!" She turned to Solana. "How about if you tell me the story?"

"Good idea." Solana shot her friends a "we'll discuss this later" look before beginning her uncle's saga. She told Ellie everything, starting with the accident, skipping the part about her being partly responsible. Ellie listened intently, obviously taking Solana and the problem seriously. "I'm sure the pond would qualify as a wetland," Solana told her, finally.

"Solana saw a boreal toad at the pond," Becca piped in. "Those are endangered in Colorado."

Solana glared at Becca, resting a hand on her hip. "As if she doesn't know that already."

Ellie leaned her head back and laughed. Mr. P. hopped off her lap and slunk into the adjoining room. She cleared her throat, regaining her composure. "I'm always impressed with land that attracts an endangered species. But actually, right now I'm most interested in open space. How many acres does your uncle have?"

Solana thought. "Over a hundred—maybe two. The ranch is huge."

Ellie raised her eyebrows. "Where is it located?"

Solana told her.

Ellie crossed one leg over the other and leaned back. "Does your uncle know you're here, Solana?"

Solana's heart sank as she shook her head. She waited for Ellie to kick them all out of the room. Instead Ellie stood and gathered a stack of pamphlets, booklets, and papers from a rack beside her desk.

"Give these to your uncle and have him call me," Ellie instructed. "His ranch has possibilities from what you've told me."

Solana wanted to reach out and hug Ellie. She took the stack of information and clutched it to her chest. "Really?"

Ellie smiled. "Oh, yes—that is, if he's interested. But I need to visit the property, so have him call me soon, okay? Land protection can be quite a process."

Solana nodded, unable to remove the grin from her face. Manuel would be so happy. Her friends exchanged smiles. Becca and Tyler high-fived.

Becca whispered, "We did it."

"Thank you very much," Solana said. She reached out and shook Ellie's hand again.

"Glad I could help."

Solana and her friends turned to go. Before Solana shut the door, Ellie called for her.

"Can I talk to you alone for a minute?" Ellie motioned for Solana to come back into the office.

Solana turned to her friends. "I'll be right there."

She stepped into the office and shut the door behind her. Ellie led her to the table. "I heard you explaining some of these photos and samples to your friends."

Solana jumped inside. They were probably supposed to leave everything alone. "Is that okay?"

"Of course." She put on a pair of reading glasses that hung from a beaded chain around her neck. "I was impressed with your knowledge."

"Science is my passion."

"Well, it shows." Ellie picked up the photo of the bird that had caught Becca's interest. "That's why I thought you'd be interested in knowing—this is actually a *male* golden-crowned kinglet, not a female." She pointed to the bird's head. "See, the males have an orange crown—the females have yellow."

Solana studied the details and committed them to memory. "Okay, thanks." She looked at Ellie's wise face and smiled.

Ellie pointed to the feather near the picture. "And you were right—this is a kinglet feather, but it's from a ruby-crowned kinglet."

Solana nodded, wishing her friends weren't waiting outside so she could stick around and learn more about the other specimens on the table. There were many that she was dying to ask Ellie about.

"I didn't want to embarrass you in front of your friends." Ellie removed her glasses. "But I figured you'd want to know the correct information."

"I do."

"Oh, you'll love this." Ellie walked to the other side of the table. She picked up another photo. "Look what I saw not far from here when I was out hiking last weekend." She handed Solana the photo. "Isn't he gorgeous?"

Solana gasped. "A lynx?" Solana was suddenly lost in the golden eyes of the beautiful gray creature. How amazing to make a career out of finding and studying things like this, and working to protect them! "I can't believe you were able to get so close to him."

"Actually I was hiding behind a bush. I had my good camera with me."

"I read that they were bringing some lynx down from Canada,

but I never expected to see one in Copper Ridge."

"Neither did I. Hopefully we'll see more in the future."

Solana handed the picture back to Ellie. "Thanks for showing me this. It's amazing." Once again she remembered her friends. "I better get going."

Ellie walked Solana to the door. Before opening it she grabbed another booklet. "Take this—it's full of details about wildlife in the Rocky Mountains—you'll love it." She held the door for Solana. "I hope to see you again."

"I'm sure you will." Solana waved good-bye to Ellie. She headed for the stairs.

Jacie, Becca, and Hannah were sitting on the bottom few steps. Tyler leaned against the wall. "You took long enough," he said when he saw Solana.

"I owe you big for finding this place, Ty." Her tattoo itched. She carefully scratched it through her T-shirt sleeve. *Maybe this secret tribute to the ranch will become a reminder of how I saved it.*

chapter 10

"I can't believe this day." Solana poured another scoop of grain into Carmen's feed bag, stroking the horse as Carmen bent to eat. She, Becca, Jacie, and Hannah had been helping at the ranch all afternoon, but her mind was more on the conservancy than on the horses. "I can't wait to go home and read the information Ellie gave us."

"Now aren't you glad you listened to me?" Becca stroked Shadow's nose and held a handful of grain out to him.

"Yeah, yeah, Becca," Solana said. "You were right, once again."

Becca tossed her ponytail. "As usual."

Solana carried the grain to the next horse. "But you aren't prideful about it or anything. That's good to know."

Jacie set her broom against the wall. "I never expected to spend the rest of my summer saving the earth."

"Me neither." Hannah shook her head and smiled. "God sure does work in mysterious ways."

Solana looked at Hannah. "So, you really think it was God who led us to Ellie, huh? All this time I thought it was Tyler, the king of Internet research." She'd been rationalizing it in her mind all afternoon, trying to convince herself that finding the article, Tyler's success on the Internet, and their meeting with Ellie were simply good timing. "And I'm the one who stayed up all night researching."

"Think about it," Becca said. "Circumstances don't fall into place this perfectly."

Solana shrugged. "Maybe I'll believe you if our new plan works like we want it to." She looked around. They didn't have time to speculate on God's involvement. "We have to get this place cleaned up before Ellie visits." She shoved an empty wheelbarrow into a corner. "Too bad Tyler had to go home and help his dad so early. We could use a set of male hands." She picked up the grain bag and set it against the wall. Through the window she spotted Ramón strolling toward the stable with a super-sized soda in one hand. He took a quick drink then waved to Solana. She waved back. Should she tell him about the conservancy? Maybe he'd want to help, since he'd been left out of the fund-raisers. He'd probably be as excited as she and her friends were about the idea. But what if he wanted to know details about The Greenhouse and about Ellie? They didn't know anything yet. It might be better to wait until she read all the pamphlets and the details were worked out.

When Ramón entered the stable, he looked around. "Wow, you guys have been busy. I guess I can go home now."

Solana smiled proudly. She wiped her sweaty brow, envying Ramón's cold drink. When they were dating, she wouldn't have thought twice about asking him for a sip. "We figured since you were so swamped, we'd get as much done as possible."

"Great." Ramón's grateful smile seemed stiff and tired. "I really appreciate it." He leaned back on his heels and took a deep breath. "Um, Solana, can I talk to you?"

"Sure."

He gave Becca, Jacie, and Hannah a quick look, like he wanted them to leave but couldn't bring himself to say it without sounding rude.

"Uh." Ramón cleared his throat. "Can we go outside or something? It's about your uncle."

"You can tell us what's going on," Becca said politely. "Solana will tell us anyway."

"True." Ramón looked at Solana. "Do you mind if they stay?"

Solana studied her friends' faces. They weren't usually so pushy. Did they not trust her alone with Ramón? What did they think she and Ramón would do? But when they all took a step closer to her, surrounding her like a small protective army, she caught on to why they wanted to stay. The last thing she needed was one more moment alone with Ramón to leave her confused and depressed.

"It's okay," Solana said, thankful for Becca's and Hannah's concern. "If it's about *Tío* Manuel they might as well hear. They're practically family."

Ramón hesitated. "Okay." He licked his lips. Why was he stalling? "I went to see Manuel today."

"How is he?" Hannah asked.

"Good, considering all his body has been through. But you know Manuel. He's tough." Ramón went on for a while about Manuel's physical therapy. As Solana listened she sensed that he was only using it as an excuse to put off sharing more important news. Something in his eyes said that she might not want to hear it. But with all the emotional ups and downs of the last few weeks, she couldn't stand waiting.

"If he's doing so well, why do you look worried?" Solana asked before he could change the subject again.

Ramón set his drink down and glanced out the window. "Is Maricella around here?"

Solana shook her head. "She's in the house."

Ramón scratched his head. He lowered his voice. "They missed the loan payment for August."

Solana's heart sank. She could almost hear time ticking away on a giant cosmic clock.

"Don't loan companies allow you to skip a payment if there's an emergency?" Becca asked.

Ramón, Solana, Jacie, and Hannah all looked at Becca, puzzled about how she'd know something like that.

"I overheard some men talking at the community center once," she explained. "There's a lot of talk about financial problems around that place."

Ramón leaned against the wall. "Skipping a payment might be possible, but Manuel's stuck in the hospital with bills piling up every time a nurse brings him an aspirin or changes a bandage. This morning he tried to go without his pain medicine because he found out how much each pill costs. I was there when Maricella saw him and found out what he was doing. She really laid into him." Ramón sighed. "I didn't know Maricella could get so mad. She's usually so quiet."

Solana smiled, remembering the first time she'd found out about her aunt's hidden temper the hard way. "She's quiet until you get to know her."

Ramón's face turned serious again. "Manuel plans to send the payment late and pay the penalty, but he's already worried about next month."

Jacie rubbed her lips together, thinking hard. "What about the money from the fund-raisers?"

"Some medical expenses have already started coming—like the ambulance fee—so Maricella has been using the money for that."

"And it'll be harder to keep up once the hospital costs start coming in," Hannah said sadly.

Solana's stomach tightened. But remembering the brochures in her bedroom at home, she chased the fear away. Manuel would not miss his next payment—not if she had anything to do with it. He couldn't miss it. "Don't worry, Ramón. It's going to work out."

Ramón squinted in confusion. "What are you talking about? Once he gets out of the hospital, he won't be able to work right away—it'll be months before he's a hundred percent. Unless he has an extremely understanding loan officer, they'll probably foreclose if he can't pay the bill."

"That is *not* going to happen." Solana stood up. She looked at her friends for backup. "Trust me."

chapter 11

"Wow." Becca sat cross-legged on Solana's bed. She turned over the brochure in her hand to read the other side. "These conservancies are interesting."

"The Greenhouse is responsible for almost all of the protected open space in Copper Ridge," Hannah said. "You'd never guess that by looking at the office."

"Or by looking at Ellie." Solana held up the paper she'd been reading. "This tells about a historical house outside Copper Ridge that was bought by The Greenhouse. It has over 50 acres of marshland on the property. The list of animals that benefit from the marsh goes on and on." She handed the paper to Becca to read.

"Oh—Rothchild Manor. We took a field trip to that place in sixth grade," Becca said. "Remember, Jace?"

Jacie looked over Becca's shoulder. "Yeah, it was so creepy." Jacie shivered.

"That's because it's haunted." Solana moved closer to Jacie. "And anyone who touches anything in the house is tormented by a ghost for the rest of her life." Solana grabbed the back of Jacie's neck and let out a piercing screech. Jacie jumped about three feet off the bed and screamed. Solana laughed and couldn't stop, even when Jacie threw a pillow at her.

"You know I don't believe in that garbage." Jacie rubbed the back of her neck, red-faced from embarrassment.

"Then why did you jump?" Solana lunged at Jacie again.

"Knock it off!" Jacie said through her teeth.

"Now children." Hannah tossed another brochure into Solana's lap. "We have a lot of reading to do."

"Yes, Master." Solana opened the brochure. "I'm just so excited over all of this stuff that I can't control my actions."

"It looks like the hardest part of wildlife and land protection is getting funding." Becca leaned against Solana's headboard.

Solana covered her face and groaned. "Money, our eternal problem."

"I bet they get a lot of their funds from grants. My mom writes grant proposals, requesting money from big organizations all the time. How do you think they keep the community center going? I bet she'd write one for you if you need it."

"Can you ask her?"

"Sure, or she can teach you how to write a proposal of your own." Becca laid down her booklet. "I wonder if the conservancy will do something with Manuel's ranch similar to what they did with Rothchild Manor."

Solana shook her head. "I doubt it. The Rothchilds have been dead for decades—that's why their house was turned into a museum."

Becca hopped up from the bed. "But Solana, wouldn't it be cool if your uncle's ranch became something like Rothchild Manor—a place for people to visit and take kids on field trips. Try to picture it."

Hannah's eyes lit up. "Or a place for parties like the one we had for Alvaro. Your uncle was great with the kids—it was obvious he loved every minute of it. He could have children visit, ride the horses, and learn about ranch life."

"We could all work there." Becca started pacing back and forth.

Solana laid down her stack of papers. "I never thought about anything like that." She pictured her uncle with a line of children waiting to ride horses—teaching them how to sit properly and hold the reins.

"He might like that, now that his own kids are grown up," Hannah suggested. "And like Ramón said, he won't be able to do any heavy work around the ranch for a while. This would give him something to do."

Jacie bit her bottom lip, staring at the picture of Rothchild Manor. "But is that what your uncle wants, Solana—to turn his ranch into a tourist attraction?"

"Why wouldn't he?" Becca bounced back onto the bed. "It would be something new and exciting."

Solana rested her chin in her hand and thought. Would Manuel want new and exciting? He'd never mentioned wanting to do anything except raise horses. But then he'd never faced losing his ranch before. If he had to choose between losing his home and turning it into a park, wouldn't he choose to keep it? He'd *have* to choose to keep it. The ranch was important to him—to the entire family. "I'm sure my uncle will be open to anything." She gathered the pamphlets and set them aside. "At least the ranch would still be there."

"Besides," Becca said, sitting down again, "the conservancy people will probably be the ones to decide what happens to the ranch. They'll help him come up with some great possibilities."

● ● ●

dragonfly on my shoulder

"See you tomorrow," Solana called from the front door as her friends jumped into Jacie's car. She watched them drive off before going back inside.

Her stomach growled. How long had it been since she'd eaten? She'd grabbed a quick lunch at the ranch, but nothing since then. Maybe she could talk Mamá into making tamales for supper.

Her parents met her in the hallway, turned her around, and led her to the living room.

"So," Papá said, "what were you and your friends up to this afternoon? You were upstairs for a long time."

"Oh." Solana shrugged. "We were just hanging out."

Mamá eyed Solana. "Usually you and your friends hang out in the kitchen when you are here—Tyler always talks me into making something to eat."

Solana threw up her arms. "Well, Tyler wasn't here today. His dad had a ton of work for him to do at home—and we girls weren't hungry."

"After a day of working at the ranch?" Mamá crossed her arms. "Usually you're starving."

Papá leaned close to his wife's ear. "Maybe they're all on diets."

Solana strolled toward the couch. "Well, school *is* starting soon. We want to look good in our jeans."

"Mmhm," Mamá mumbled.

Papá rested his hand gently on Solana's arm and directed her to sit. "Let's talk, *mi'ja*."

Solana sat. She kicked her sandals off so she could put her feet up on the couch. Despite her effort to stop herself, she yawned.

"You look tired." Mamá sat beside Solana. "You have dark circles under your eyes. You go to the ranch too much. Tomorrow you stay home and get some rest."

"I'm fine," Solana insisted. "I'll get to bed early tonight, I promise."

Papá leaned forward, his large brown eyes focused on Solana's face. "Solana, you have been at the ranch every day since the accident. You and your friends made all that money to help Manuel and Maricella. That was a great thing, and the family is grateful to you." He looked at his wife then back at Solana. "Now, you are up to something else I think."

Solana shifted her eyes from one parent to another. She tried to come up with another excuse but her mind was too tired. She smiled innocently. "What makes you think that?"

"Just the way you and your friends were acting this afternoon— very secretive," Mamá said. "And I heard you up in the middle of the night on the computer. You were on the phone before the sun came up."

Solana twisted her watchband, trying to come up with something to satisfy her parents. Would it be so awful if they knew about the conservancy? They'd find out eventually. No—what if they told her to forget the whole thing? But they'd only keep prodding if she insisted nothing was going on. "Okay, I admit it. I'm still looking for a way to help Manuel."

"Oh, Solana," Mamá groaned.

"I can't give up on him, Mamá."

Papá heaved an exasperated sigh. "None of us wants to give up on Manuel."

Solana lowered her gaze. From the sound of her father's voice, she sensed that he thought she was trying to make up for the rest of the family not trying hard enough. Papá was at the ranch every weekend and sometimes after work. No way did she want him to feel like he wasn't doing his share.

"I can't stop looking for possibilities. I have time to do it, with school out." Solana sat up straighter and took her feet off the couch. "And don't say that I'm just a kid, or that it isn't my job, please."

Papá raised his voice slightly. "We just do not want to see you wear yourself out only to be disappointed."

"I won't." Solana felt a fresh rush of determination well up inside of her. "*Familia* always helps each other out—I've heard you say it a million times—it's the only thing that lasts."

Papá shook his head like he always did when one of the kids threw one of his lines back at him.

"So, I *can't* give up. And if it doesn't work out, I promise not to be devastated." That part was a lie—she knew it, but it seemed like a necessary one. "At least I'll know I tried everything."

Mamá cupped Solana's chin in her hand. "Okay, as long as you remember that no matter how hard you try, Manuel could still lose the ranch. Some things are just not meant to work out."

"He won't lose it," Solana assured her mother and herself. *He can't.*

● ● ●

Becca's words crept into Solana's dreams in the middle of the night. "The conservancy will probably decide what happens to the ranch."

Solana's eyes popped open. Large invisible hands grabbed her heart and squeezed. What if Manuel didn't have a choice about what happened to his land? What if the people from The Greenhouse kicked him off his land and turned it into one of those tacky dude ranches or something else completely under their control?

Then she remembered Ellie. Ellie didn't seem like the type to tear a family away from their home. Then again . . .

She stared at the ceiling. *I am not going to freak out about this. It's the best possibility we've come up with. If Hannah and Becca were right— that God is pulling this whole thing together—then He'd never throw in a curve like that—not if He's really on my side.*

And then it hit her. Why would God be on her side in the first place? What had she ever done for Him?

Nothing. Absolutely nothing.

chapter 12

Solana poked her head inside The Greenhouse office. "Hello!" She walked in and looked around for Ellie. Mr. Peabody meowed from his spot on the office chair. Solana walked over and stroked his soft, gray fur.

Ellie hurried in from the other room. Her reading glasses balanced on the end of her nose.

"Oh, hello, Solana." She dropped an armload of stuffed file folders onto her desk and let out a heavy sigh. The top folder slipped from the pile. A shower of photos and Internet printouts fell to the floor and scattered. "Great," Ellie muttered. She stooped down to gather them.

Solana knelt down to help. She wanted to stop and read each page that she picked up, but observing Ellie's haste in gathering her material, she pushed her curiosity aside. "Do these go in any particular order?" She searched the sheets for page numbers.

"Not at the moment." Ellie took the papers Solana held out to her and returned them to the folder. "Thanks for the help."

Solana looked around for signs of anyone else being in the office. "Are you always alone here?"

Ellie adjusted the folders so they wouldn't fall again. "Most of the time. We have a pretty small staff. I have people out taking photos, arranging for funding, raising awareness for our projects—things I don't have time for. All of the research, the grant writing, and administrative work have been up to me lately. I finally got the okay to hire a college intern as an assistant, once the new semester starts."

Solana leaned against the sample table. "Are you connected with the University of Colorado?"

"I'm actually a professor at UC Berkeley—environmental studies. I'm on a two-year sabbatical."

Solana widened her eyes in excitement. "Really? UC Berkeley is one of the colleges I plan to apply to. How did you end up in Copper Ridge?"

"The Greenhouse needed a director and I needed a break from teaching. The former director is a friend of mine. He took a position at a wildlife reserve in Nairobi. So I'm holding down the fort here."

"Do you like it?"

How could a person go from an exciting city like Berkeley, California, to Copper Ridge? She must be bored stiff.

"I love it! Copper Ridge is beautiful—so relaxing compared to what I'm used to—and I've been involved in some really exciting projects." She patted the stack of files. "It's my dream job really, even if I have felt a bit overworked lately."

"I bet you're counting down the days until you get an intern."

"Yes. I look forward to it with great anticipation." Ellie removed her glasses and let them dangle at her chest. She put her hands on her lower back and arched backward. "So, Solana, I'm sure you didn't come all the way down here to help me chase paper across the floor. What can I do for you?"

The questions that had come up the evening before rolled off Solana's tongue with an ease that amazed even her.

Ellie went to sit on her chair and almost sat on the cat instead. "Shoo, Mr. P."

Mr. P.'s heavy paws hit the ground with a thud. He found a place in a corner under the desk, meowing loudly before curling up into a fat ball.

"Oh, he's a big whiner." Ellie peeked under the desk and made a face at Mr. P.

Solana laughed. Mr. P. meowed pathetically again and Solana stuck her tongue out at him.

"See," Ellie scolded the cat. "Nobody feels sorry for you."

"Back to your questions." Ellie leaned back in her chair. "Each conservancy has its own set of policies. When we deal with private landowners, I work out the details on a case-by-case basis. It's not common for people to want to stay, but it has been done."

"So you won't buy my uncle's ranch and then kick him off the place?"

Ellie chuckled. "No."

"What about how a person chooses to use the land? Will my uncle have to turn the ranch into a sanctuary for wild mustangs or something?"

"Not necessarily." Ellie folded her arms across her chest and thought. "We do have guidelines as far as how protected land is used. He wouldn't be able to do anything that would damage the land, water, or wildlife."

"Oh, he wouldn't anyway."

"In order to convince those who provide us with funds, the ranch would have to benefit Copper Ridge somehow, such as providing open space." Ellie gazed thoughtfully at Solana. "Solana, have you spoken to your uncle?"

Solana glanced at the floor. "Not yet."

"None of this can happen without him."

"I'm going to talk to him about it really soon." *But when? How?* She stared at the floor, her thoughts whirling. *What if this doesn't work out?* Her heart rate sped up. *It has to work.*

Solana looked at Ellie, desperate to have an answer. "I was wondering—is there any way that you can visit the ranch before I talk to Manuel? That way he won't get his hopes up, if you check out his property and then decide you aren't interested."

Ellie drummed her fingers on her desk. "I really shouldn't—not without the consent of one of your adult family members."

"I take total responsibility if anyone gets mad."

Ellie paused and stared at her desk for what seemed like forever. Finally, shaking her head, she opened a black leather appointment book. "If you were just some brainless kid I would say no in a heartbeat." She pointed her pen at Solana. "If anyone objects to me being at the ranch, I'll need to leave. Agreed?"

Solana nodded. Her heart pounded with excitement. "Agreed."

● ● ●

"What if your aunt shows up while Ellie is here?" Hannah shut the door of Jacie's green Tercel.

Jacie stopped in her tracks. "I never thought of that."

"I did." Solana watched the road for Ellie's car. "I'll introduce Ellie as a friend."

"One that you've known for a whole three days?" Jacie asked.

"Or I'll explain what we're up to. But don't worry, I'll think of something. Like I told Ellie, if anything bad happens, it's all on me."

"You bet it is," Tyler said. "I've gotten in enough trouble this summer to last me until Christmas."

"Why would Maricella get mad anyway?" Becca cut in. "We're just trying to help. It's a good plan."

Hannah twisted her ponytail, still appearing hesitant. "If Maricella arrives, maybe meeting Ellie will give her some hope for the future."

"Exactly." Hearing the sound of tires, Solana moved away from the side of Jacie's car.

A battered red jeep pulled into the driveway.

"Nice wheels," Tyler shouted as Ellie stepped out of the Jeep in baggy denim shorts, a striped men's shirt, and her wavy hair pulled back in clips. She raised a hand in greeting.

Solana waved at Ellie and smiled. In a moment of panic she turned to Hannah. "You have film in the camera, right?"

Hannah patted the camera that hung from a thin strap over her shoulder. "A fresh roll."

Becca grabbed Solana's shoulder and gave her a shake. "You nervous?"

"No!" She put her finger over her lips to shush Becca.

Ellie took her time walking from her Jeep. "Nice place, Solana," she said when she reached the group. Shading her eyes with her hand, she looked in the direction of the pasture. She turned in a small circle, taking in all she could see. "I should have paid more attention when I wrote down this address. It's adjacent to an open pasture we're looking to protect." She waved her hand toward some property down the road.

"That's not protected?" Solana stared at the land on which she sometimes rode the horses and where the *tesoros puros* often grazed. "I just assumed—"

"No, it's public land. Developers are currently trying to purchase it so they can fill it with small ranchettes. They buy ranches and divide them into smaller lots. It's quite a profitable endeavor.

This time they're after that open land." She looked around and sighed. "I'm not against progress, but how many more houses, malls, and grocery stores does one town need? And people forget that once land is developed, it can never be regained. Our resources are disappearing endlessly." Ellie sighed. "I'll get off my soapbox and stop boring you with my passion."

"It doesn't bother me," Solana said. "I totally agree with you."

She glanced at her watch. Maricella wasn't due home for two hours—plenty of time. "So, what do you need to see first, Ellie?"

Ellie looked around the property. "The pond where you saw the boreal toad is probably the best place to start."

Solana directed the group toward Dragonfly Pond. On the way, a picture of the *tesoros puros* flashed through her mind. What would happen to them if developers bought all the open pasture? "Would a herd of wild horses help to gain funding?" Solana blurted.

Ellie looked thoughtful. "Tell me about them."

Solana talked while Hannah snapped pictures. Ellie listened, jotting notes in a small spiral notebook she held in her hand. "I've heard of those horses. I didn't realize they came down this far. We'll see what we can do."

Tyler maneuvered his way around Hannah to walk on the other side of Solana. "What are the pictures for, Sol?"

"The conservancy sends pictures to potential donors. The guy who usually takes pictures for The Greenhouse is swamped right now, so I volunteered Hannah."

"Hannah," Tyler asked, "are they paying you well?"

Hannah snapped a picture of the stable. "I'm donating my services—*this* time."

Jacie glanced back at her. "Hannah, you are so kind."

Hannah tossed her hair. "At the end of the year I'll just write it off as a charitable donation." She laughed. "As if I ever work enough to pay taxes anyway."

"Thanks for doing this, Hannah. I really do appreciate it." Solana couldn't imagine this was the same shy, serious girl she'd met on the first day of the previous school year.

Solana turned her attention to Ellie, telling her everything she could about the ranch.

"As you can see, my uncle has some pretty large hay and grain fields. And my aunt has a really nice vegetable garden near the house," Solana explained. "Maricella grows practically every kind of pepper. She cans her own homemade salsa to sell at the fair every year—it's the best."

"I love hot salsa," Ellie said, her solemn face breaking into a wry smile. "I think *that's* something worth funding."

The tension broke and Solana laughed. "In that case I'll be sure you get some."

"Why thank you." Ellie turned to the others. "See? There are perks to this job."

"Maybe I'll reconsider my career choice," Tyler said. "A guy can't get enough home-canned salsa."

"How long have you been working for The Greenhouse, Ellie?" Jacie asked.

"Only a year," Ellie said. "But I've been involved in land preservation for a long time. It's very important to me to protect creation." She waved her hand, toward the sky then around, encouraging everyone to look at the surrounding trees, fields, and vegetation. "God gave us all this beauty to enjoy. But it's also our responsibility to care for it and see that it lasts."

Solana took a long look at Ellie. *God? Is she a . . . ? No way—she's probably just using words like "God" and "creation" in a generic way. Katie Spencer and her Wicca friends talked about God all the time and they weren't Christians.*

In her typical fashion, Hannah quickly responded to the spiritual buzzwords. "Ellie, are you a Christian?"

Ellie smiled. "Yes."

Solana sighed. *Great*. But then, she considered Ellie's earthiness, her knowledge of science, and interest in the environment. Solana had never thought of Christians belonging in her world of science. Yet Ellie was what Solana aspired to be—*and* she was a Christian.

"I had a feeling that you were," Becca said.

Tyler caught up with Ellie. "So did I."

What gave it away? Solana wanted to ask. What kind of evidence did Christians look for that told them, "Hey, I think she's one of us"?

Her friends flooded Ellie with spiritual questions, dominating the conversation. *Could Ellie pay attention to her job with them yammering at her?*

"Are there other Christians at the conservancy?" Jacie asked.

Ellie shook her head. "That's the hard part about my job. Everyone at the office sees me as an extremist freak—not that we have a lot of time to sit around debating about such things. It's a shame so many people see science and God as mutually exclusive. In my eyes, science and working with the environment only proves they are interconnected. My work strengthens my belief, continually reminding me what a creative and complex God rules the universe."

As hard as she tried, Solana couldn't ignore the conversation taking place around her. The question of creation versus more scientific theories had always baffled her. Since childhood she had claimed to believe in evolution. But then there were times when the idea of a Creator made sense too.

"Solana isn't a believer," Hannah said quietly.

"You don't need to whisper," Solana said. "It's not like my beliefs, or lack of, are a big secret around here."

"Guess what. I haven't always been a believer either. At one time I was exactly like my co-workers. It took God a long time to break through to this stubborn old woman's heart." She smiled at Solana.

Solana smiled back. "You're not old."

Ellie laughed. "If you only knew."

Solana listened as Ellie and her friends pointed out specific things in nature that reminded them of God, or proved that the world could have only come from a divine Creator. Ellie sounded a little different than Solana's friends—maybe because she understood what it felt like to *not* believe.

"I'm so glad that you're a Christian," Hannah said. "It makes this whole thing seem as though God's hand is in it even more."

"Well, I do hope that I can help Solana's uncle."

When they arrived at their destination, Solana cupped her hands around her mouth. "Okay, Mr. Boreal Toad," she shouted. "Come on out! Don't let me down."

Becca snorted and whispered to Jacie and Tyler. "I'm picturing a bunch of little toads huddled in the hollow of an old log, like the mice in *Cinderella*."

Tyler croaked, "We can do it, we can do it, we can help our friend Solana."

Solana turned to Ellie, pointing at her friends. "See what I put up with?"

"Yeah." Ellie nodded. "You poor thing." She looked around, her hands resting on her hips. "This is quite lovely. Somewhat unique."

Solana stood back with her friends while Ellie surveyed the area. Did she think it held possibilities? Was she finding what she hoped for?

"This is a natural pond," Solana said, "not man-made."

"I can tell." Ellie crouched down and looked more closely at the water. She glanced back at Solana. "I see that boreal toad you mentioned. There are a few of them, actually."

Solana scurried over. "Where?" The others followed.

Ellie pointed to a small toad sitting near a bunch of reeds, then another that hid under a log.

"So we do have something to protect." Solana squatted to examine the toads, much more eager to see them today than when Jacie had pointed one of them out.

"You sure do." Ellie stood up. "Like I said, I'm after open space. But having an endangered species certainly helps when it comes to asking for donations."

"So what's the next step?" Solana followed Ellie, who took a notebook out of her pocket and started jotting down notes. Solana tried to peek over Ellie's shoulder, without making it obvious, but couldn't make out any of her notes.

"First I need to test the pond water for any harmful fungus or organism." Ellie finished writing. "I'll need to speak with the rest of the staff regarding my findings, show the pictures, and discuss the benefits of protecting a ranch like this one." She pointed to Solana. "But before I take one more step, I need your uncle's permission."

"I'll talk to him tonight," Solana promised.

Ellie took another look around. "It's time I head back." She turned to Hannah. "Get that film to me as soon as you can. We'll reimburse you for the developing."

Hannah shook her head. "That's okay. Solana's worth it."

Solana glanced over her shoulder, dumbfounded. "Another charitable donation?"

"No, a gift."

"Oh." Solana grinned at Hannah. "Thanks."

"You sure have an amazing bunch of friends, Solana." Ellie patted Solana on the back. "I wish I had been so fortunate as a teenager."

"Yeah." Solana looked at each of her friends. "They're good kids."

On the walk back they all talked more about the new possibilities for the ranch. According to Ellie, the hay Manuel grew would be a plus because it was a benefit to wetlands. The fact that the property was so close to land the conservancy was already working to protect would help tremendously.

This is great, Solana said to herself. *We can't lose.*

Before they reached the house Tyler tapped Solana on the arm and whispered, "Ramón just drove up."

Solana jumped inside. "Great."

Becca groaned. "Uh-oh. How are you going to explain this?"

Ramón stepped out of his car and casually approached the group. "Hey, guys." He reached his hand out to Ellie. "Hi, I'm Ramón. And you are—"

chapter 13

Ramón leaned on the porch rail and looked out toward the stable. After a moment he looked back at Solana, a dozen questions in his eyes. He rubbed Ellie's business card between his fingers. "Why didn't you tell me about this before, Solana?"

Hannah and Jacie sat on the porch swing. Tyler and Becca sat at the patio table, looking awkwardly at each other, like they wanted to say something but knew they'd better keep quiet.

Solana got up from her chair. "I wanted to make sure it was going to work out first."

Ellie had handled meeting Ramón so professionally, politely shaking his hand, offering her card, and leaving. But now Solana almost wished she had stuck around to explain more about the conservancy to Ramón.

Ramón threw up his arms, shaking his head. "It's a great idea,

Solana, but you can't do something this huge behind your aunt's and uncle's backs."

She smiled innocently. "I'll tell Manuel all about it tonight when I visit him."

Ramón fell silent again, once more staring thoughtfully over the porch rail. Solana couldn't help noticing how cute he looked. She missed watching him in his moments of deep thought. But what was going through his head? Was he angry with her? Would it change her mind if he were?

Please, Ramón, be on my side.

The squeak of the porch swing cut through the tense silence.

"I know I shouldn't be saying this." Ramón kept his eyes on some faraway object. "Manuel trusts me to hold things together around here until he gets home. So I feel extra responsible." He turned to Solana. "But I say go for it. Nobody else has the energy or the time to come up with a better idea. And I can't stand the idea of your family losing this place." He paused, pressing his lips together. "You're sure this Ellie is legitimate? Some environmental groups can be pretty fanatical."

"Not Ellie." Solana stood at Ramón's side. "I checked everything out. She wants to work with Manuel and Maricella." She told him all about her talk with Ellie. An involuntary smile spread across her lips when she saw Ramón beginning to relax. She should have known that Ramón would see how perfect this solution was. "I'll lend you the information I have on The Greenhouse. That way you can see what they are all about."

Ramón tapped the railing with the side of his fist. "The yearly bill for the homeowner's insurance came today. I thought your aunt was going to burst into tears when she saw it." He sighed. "I guess she's been so busy that she forgot about it. Perfect timing, huh?"

Solana shoved her hair out of her face, wanting to tear it out. "See? We can't wait any longer."

Ramón patted Solana's shoulder. Her arm tingled. "I think Manuel's ready to try anything at this point."

"So why wouldn't he be excited about the idea?"

"I hope he is." Ramón walked slowly down the steps.

Solana watched him disappear into the stable. She plopped into the porch swing between Jacie and Hannah, releasing a loud sigh of relief. "Yes!"

"I thought we'd blown it for sure." Becca looked toward the stable. "Now the trick is convincing your uncle."

Solana lunged forward. "You heard Ramón. Manuel is desperate." She sprang from the swing. "Come on. Let's get that film developed first. We'll do the one-hour deal so Ellie can have the pictures today. Then I'll go talk to my uncle alone."

● ● ●

"I can't believe how quick they were." Hannah flipped through her stack of photos. "One-hour developing is hardly one hour anymore."

"See?" Solana bubbled with joy, but it was mixed with nervousness, the closer she came to the moment when she would try to sell her uncle on the idea. "This is meant to be." She jumped into the front seat of Jacie's car and pointed toward the parking lot exit. "To the conservancy, James."

Jacie lowered her voice to sound like a man. "Yes, sir."

Within minutes they were flooding the office of The Greenhouse. A tall, gangly man with graying curly hair looked at the group as if they were a gang of thugs.

"Excuse me," he stammered. "I think you have the wrong building."

To Solana's relief, Ellie appeared in the doorway. "It's okay, Dwayne, they're with me."

Dwayne gave the kids one more suspicious look before taking his project into the other room.

"So, what do you have for me?" Ellie took the pictures Solana held out to her.

"They turned out great," Solana said.

While Ellie thumbed through the pictures, Solana took a look around, to see if there was anything new in the office. On Ellie's desk she spotted a framed photo of a young woman with waist-length, wavy hair. Her face looked familiar. Maybe Ellie had a daughter. The woman in the picture was dressed in a headband, a tie-dyed T-shirt, and tattered bell-bottomed jeans. Around her neck were several strings of beads. A Halloween costume? A young man with stringy hair and an overgrown mustache had his arm around her.

"Who's this?" She held the picture out to Ellie.

"Oh, that's me." Ellie took off her glasses. "Isn't that a riot? I found it in a drawer at home and brought it here to give everyone a good laugh."

Solana looked again as the others gathered around.

"That's you?" Jacie's mouth fell open.

Tyler grabbed the picture. "No way!"

Ellie laughed even harder. "Can you believe it?"

Hannah looked over Tyler's shoulder, then at Ellie. "You look so . . . different."

"Yeah." She settled back in her chair. "When I look at that picture I feel like I'm seeing a completely different person. Sometimes I can still smell the patchouli incense and lack of deodorant."

Jacie and Becca wrinkled their faces in disgust.

"You don't look like an 'Ellie' in this picture," Solana said, pointing to the photo.

"Well," Ellie chuckled. "I didn't go by Ellie back then."

Solana raised her eyebrows. "You look even less like an 'Eleanor.'"

Ellie raised her eyebrows in return. "That's because I was 'Petal.'"

Becca's eyes grew wide. "That was your name?"

"Yep." Ellie smiled proudly. "Back in my wild hippie days. Like it?"

Everyone looked at each other and laughed.

Tyler turned the photo around and pointed to the man. "So, who's the guy—Stem?"

Ellie got up and grabbed the picture, nudging Tyler. "No, funny guy—that's Alec, my husband. He wasn't my husband then of course. That picture was taken while we were serving in the Peace Corps."

"Is that where you met?"

Ellie nodded. She stroked the string of beads that held her glasses around her neck.

Hannah stared at the photo. "But didn't hippies take drugs and . . . things like that?"

"Most of us. I told you God had to work hard." She sat back down, crossed her ankles, and stretched out her legs. "My poor parents. They were as conservative as you can get. They raised me in church and with strong Christian values, but I didn't want anything to do with it. I thought a person should choose her own way. I chose my own way all right—and learned some tough lessons. But God persisted." She grinned. "I'm so glad He did."

Solana couldn't stop looking at the photo. So at one time Ellie and been like . . . like her in a way. Not that she planned to join the Peace Corps or take drugs.

Jacie pointed to the picture again. "Those beads are like the ones you're wearing now."

Ellie nodded. "Genuine love beads, my friend. Alec made them for me as an engagement gift."

Becca and Tyler looked at each other. "Aw."

Ellie continued. "After he died I had them made into this." She pulled gently on the beaded strand around her neck.

"When did you give your life to Christ?" Hannah asked.

Ellie cleared her throat. Her voice became distant and sad. "About a year after Alec died. You know, that is one of my biggest regrets—I have others of course—but I can't help thinking that if I'd only heard God sooner, Alec might have accepted Christ too. I hate that he died without—" Her voice broke.

"Don't forget it had nothing to do with you," Hannah said. "God gives everyone a chance to accept or reject Him."

"Of course. But I can't help the regret . . ."

Hannah nodded, taking another long look at the photo.

Solana leaned against the table listening. Had Ellie turned to God because she was lonely without her husband? Or suddenly afraid of death? She remembered how needy she had felt for some kind of spirituality after losing Ramón, then again after coming so close to drowning on the rock-climbing trip with Becca. Did Ellie try other religions first? She pushed away the questions. *This is not why we're here!*

"What do you think of the pictures?" she urged, pushing the photos toward Ellie.

Ellie grabbed her glasses. "Right. The pictures." She picked up the stack and began to flip through them. "Well done, Hannah. I'll have to keep your skills in mind the next time our photographers are busy."

Hannah blushed. "Thank you," she said, her voice soft.

Ellie took a picture from the stack and smiled. "How could I forget?" she chastised herself. She turned to Solana. "When I got back to the office there was a message on the recorder. The funding for that open pasture near your uncle's ranch came through."

"So no one can build on it? It's protected for good?"

"Almost. We still have a bit of a fight on our hands. But getting the funding is a big step." Ellie's eyes sparkled. "This means the conservancy will have an even greater interest in your uncle's ranch. That is if he's interested."

"He will be." Solana felt the excitement bubble up inside of her. "I'm sure of it."

chapter 14

"Hi, Renee." Solana waved to the nurse coming out of Manuel's room. "How's my uncle today?"

"Pretty well." The nurse smiled. "I think he pushed himself a little too hard in therapy today. I went into his room a minute ago and he looked worn out."

"We Luzes are famous for pushing ourselves. It's in our blood."

Renee continued down the hall. Solana stopped at Manuel's door and searched her purse for the card Ellie had given her. Maybe he would perk up a little after hearing there was hope for his ranch.

"*Buenas tardes,*" Solana said as she walked in. She found her uncle reclined on the bed, staring at the television he had turned to the local Spanish station. One cast-covered leg was propped up on a stack of pillows. "Now here's something I don't see every day. You vegging in front of the TV."

"Nothing but garbage on during the day." Manuel smiled

wearily at Solana. "But I run out of things to do around here."

Solana looked around the room and spotted a wheelchair in the corner. When she pictured her usually strong, independent uncle riding around in it, her soul ached. At least he wouldn't need it forever. "I can help you into the wheelchair and we can take a walk if you want."

Manuel shook his head. "I hate riding around in that thing. Makes me feel like ..." He gazed up, searching for the correct word. "Like an invalid."

"You mean 'person with a disability.' After all, you do want to be politically correct, don't you? Especially in this ward of the hospital." Solana sat in the chair beside her uncle's bed. "So, where's your roommate?"

"At his therapy session." Manuel raised his bed up a bit more and lowered the volume on the television. "So, how are you?"

"Great." Solana gave him a quick update on the horses, trying to figure out exactly how to work in the news about Ellie and the conservancy.

"I met a lady the other day," she finally said. "You would really like her." For a few minutes Solana went on and on about Ellie, and how amazing The Greenhouse conservancy was. She told him about some of the places they had helped protect, including the open pasture near his land. "And you won't believe this—she can also help you keep the ranch."

Manuel wrinkled his forehead, looking puzzled. "How?" He shook his head. "Solana, I cannot afford another loan."

Too excited to sit anymore, Solana jumped out of the chair. "No, it's better than that." She explained how the conservancy worked, and how interested Ellie was in the property.

"Dragonfly Pond is a wetland," Solana explained, unable to stop the flow of speech long enough for Manuel to get a word in. "You have an endangered species right there on your land—did you know that?"

Manuel shook his head again, staring at Solana in a way that made it impossible for her to read his thoughts. "No, I never thought to look."

Solana studied his face. Why didn't he look happy? Maybe he was just taking it all in. Or maybe he was just worn out, like the nurse said. She told him what Ellie had said about the surrounding farms being sold for ranchettes.

"Ellie loves your ranch, *Tio* Manuel. She's sending the pictures we took this morning to—"

"Whoa," Manuel cut her off. "You mean this Ellie has been to the ranch already? And she took pictures?"

"Actually Hannah took the pictures." She handed Ellie's card to Manuel. "Now she needs to do some testing on Dragonfly Pond. But she can't do anything else without your permission, so you need to call her right away."

Manuel threw up his arms. "Well, she has already done plenty without my permission. Why not testing, too?" He muttered in Spanish about how he should have known things would fall apart with him away from the ranch.

Solana stood still, stunned. What did he mean, "falling apart"? What was falling apart? She, Ramón, and her friends had been knocking themselves out so things *wouldn't* fall apart.

Manuel looked straight at her, frustration burning in his eyes. "Solana, how could you do this without asking me?"

"Because I wanted to help. I didn't want to get your hopes up if it wasn't going to work out, so I—"

"So you invited a strange woman to my property, to take pictures of everything, so she can pass them on to who knows who?"

"The people at The Greenhouse are totally trustworthy."

"Even if I did let them buy it, what would happen to your aunt and me?"

"Ellie says you can live at the ranch if you want to."

"Oh, how sweet of her. I can live at the ranch while she tells me how to run it, what I can grow, what to feed the horses."

"But she said—"

Manuel shouted, "The ranch is *my* home. I will do with it as I please!"

"But I'm trying to keep you from losing it."

"Do you think I want to lose it? That is all I think about while I am stuck in this hospital." Manuel punched the mattress. "Some things can't be helped. And sometimes what's best is the only thing that can be done. So stay out of it, Solana."

Solana took a step back. His anger caught her so off guard that she couldn't think of one thing to say. Should she tell him that Ramón liked the idea, or would that make him angrier? What could she add that would help?

"I am taking care of things my way," Manuel said, fighting for control. "Now, stay out of this. It's my problem, not yours."

"How have you taken care of things? Did you come up with some money?"

"No," Manuel snapped.

Solana twisted her purse strap. "What did you do?"

He took a deep breath. "It's not your business."

Feeling the threat of tears, she looked away from her uncle. "I better go. You need to rest."

She turned and left quickly, without a response from Manuel. She almost collided with a nurse when she rushed toward the exit, not wanting anyone to see her crying. Once inside Mamá's car, she sat in the driver's seat wondering where to go next.

● ● ●

"Solana, I'm so sorry." Becca handed Solana another tissue. "Your uncle's probably just upset because you caught him off guard. I'm sure once he calms down . . ."

Solana shook her head hard. She wiped away a stream of tears and blew her nose. "I've never seen him so mad—not at me anyway. And now we've lost the whole deal with Ellie."

"Maybe we haven't."

"You heard her." Solana heaved the balled-up tissue into Becca's trash can. "She can't do anything more without his permission." She let her hands fall to her lap. "And it all seemed so perfect."

"I know," Becca said softly. She left the box of tissue on her bed and walked over to her desk. "But, let's not give up hope yet, okay?"

Solana lay back on the bed. "The whole way over here I was racking my brain for ideas—ways to convince my uncle that the conservancy is the best solution, new things we could do to make money, like writing support letters or something. But it's like there was this voice in my head saying, 'Forget it. It's hopeless.' Maybe that's the voice of reality."

"Or the voice of the one who wants us to give up on God when we've been praying hard for something and doing everything we can to make it happen."

Solana groaned. "Oh please." *I haven't been praying. You have. So why would that "voice" bother to talk to me?*

Becca sat in the chair by her desk. She rested her elbows on her knees, chin in hand. "Your uncle told you he's taking care of it. Maybe that's a *good* thing."

Solana draped her arm over her forehead, exhausted from think-ing and crying. "I don't see how. He didn't come up with any money."

"Maybe he talked to his loan company or something, or to the hospital about a payment plan that he can afford. You never know."

Becca slapped her knee. "Well, I'm not giving up. I'm going to keep praying for things to work out."

"Fine—if it makes you feel better. It's not like I can talk you out of it." Solana closed her eyes. Was it possible that Manuel had come up with a solution? She tried to let the possibility give her new hope. But a part of her didn't even want to hope anymore—not if it would only lead to disappointment.

chapter 15

Solana shoved the push broom across the porch. Through the window she saw her aunt busying herself with housework. From the way Maricella greeted her that morning Solana felt certain that Manuel had told her everything. *All I did was try to help. Why aren't they happy?* Solana wanted to charge into the house and scream her frustrations out to her aunt. She swished the dirt off the edge of the porch.

"Hey," Ramón called from below. "Dirt doesn't make a very good shampoo."

"Sorry," Solana muttered. She plunked the broom against the side of the house and slumped down the steps.

Ramón met her at the bottom and blocked her way. She kept her focus on the ground, avoiding eye contact with him. One sweet, sympathetic look from him and it would be all over. "Do you still want help grooming the horses?"

"Yes. But first I want you to talk to me."

Solana looked away. Last night she'd felt devastated. But today the devastation was mixed with anger. Why? She didn't even know who she was mad at—her uncle for getting so mad or herself for not being able to think of a new plan. Maybe she was mad at her aunt for not at least asking about the conservancy and why Solana thought it was a good idea.

"Manuel didn't take your news very well, did he?" Ramón asked gently. For a moment it seemed like they were back to the times when she could tell him anything, without worrying about letting her guard down.

Solana nodded. "He hates the idea."

"I wish I could say I was surprised but . . ."

Solana glared up at Ramón. "What do you mean? I thought you were on my side."

"I am. The idea was great."

"If the idea was so great, then why is my uncle mad at me?" Solana fumed, fighting to keep from yelling. "And when did you suddenly decide he wouldn't go for it?"

"I just couldn't stop thinking about it after you left. I knew he'd be mad that you got Ellie involved before talking to him. Maybe if you'd done things the other way around . . ."

"I knew what I was doing. I'm not a dumb kid."

"You think I don't know that?"

"You're not acting like you know that." Solana stared at Ramón, trying to think of another comeback. No words came. She turned away. "I don't want to talk about this anymore."

"Solana, come on," Ramón called as she walked off.

● ● ●

Solana pulled her knees up to her chest and watched a bright orange dragonfly skip across the surface of the pond. She stroked her healing shoulder. How could dragonflies move so quickly and so gracefully at the same time? She couldn't manage to do anything graceful. Clumsy. Awkward. Stupid. All her efforts weren't enough.

Solana felt the familiar ache deep inside her heart.

Yesterday she and her friends had been so hopeful, and today everything was back to falling apart. And Ellie had been so sure The Greenhouse would buy the ranch.

Solana picked up a stick and poked it into the dirt in front of her. Why didn't Ramón believe in her and her idea?

She rested her forehead on her knees. *And why didn't it work out?* The angry voice of her uncle echoed in her mind. Her head felt heavy with a horrible knowledge—*I failed—again.*

A dragonfly hovered in front of her. She reached up and swatted it away. It hurt to see something so beautiful when everything, including herself, felt so ugly—as ugly as the larva she and her friends had watched on the day when they decided not to give up on the ranch.

A picture of her tattoo flashed through her mind. *I might as well have had the word* failure *tattooed on my arm.*

"'I'm going to keep praying,'" she snarled to herself, mimicking Becca. "A lot of good prayer has done so far." She looked up at the blue, cloudless sky. Was God really watching her from behind those clouds? "Are You paying attention here?" she called out. "Are You listening? If so, I have some words for You. But I don't think You'd approve of them very much."

How could her friends hold on so tightly to a God who clearly didn't care? All He'd done was give them glimpses of false hope—then snatch it away again and again. Over the last few months, Becca's, Tyler's, Jacie's, and Hannah's experiences had only strengthened their commitment to God. Wouldn't something like this make them doubt? *What keeps them going? Why pray to someone who does what He wants in the end anyway? What's the big attraction?*

She turned toward the sound of cracking twigs.

"Hey," Ramón said as he approached.

Solana turned her focus back to Dragonfly Pond. Ramón sat beside her on the ground.

"I didn't mean to upset you."

"Sorry for stomping off," Solana said, not caring that her apology didn't come out sounding very sincere.

"That's okay," Ramón said. "You've been working so hard trying to come up with ways to keep this place, and everyone jumps down your throat for it. I'd be upset too. I should have chosen my words better."

"The conservancy idea could really work, Ramón."

"Yeah, but this is Manuel's place."

"I know." Solana stared at the pasture beyond the pond. In the distance the *tesoros puros* grazed freely. Thanks to Ellie they'd graze on part of that pasture for as long as they lived—assuming everything else went through. But she wouldn't be able to sit and watch them anymore. Her throat tightened. "I just don't want to let it go."

"It means a lot to me, too."

"Does it really?"

"Solana, this is *our* place."

Solana looked into his deep dark eyes.

Ramón patted her on the arm. "So, are we friends again?"

Friends? "Yes," she said. "We're friends again." She reached out and brushed at his hair. "Sorry for giving you a dirt shampoo."

"Oh, I'll live."

As Solana stood and brushed off her jeans, she felt Ramón watching her.

"Maybe something else will work out," he said awkwardly. "You never know."

Solana looked toward the ranch house. "He did say he's taking care of things."

"Well," Ramón started toward the ranch. "Let's just hope that's a good thing."

Solana nodded. She followed Ramón. Part of her wanted to catch up to him and grab his hand. She balled her fist in resistance and closed her eyes. When she opened them, she looked toward the ranch again. A strange truck was parked in the driveway and two men were walking around the property.

"Who are those men?"

Ramón shaded his eyes to make them out. "I have no idea." He stopped and watched for a moment. "Stay here. I'll check it out."

Solana continued to follow him. "No, I want to go with you."

chapter **16**

Ramón strolled casually toward the men, Solana at his heels. "Can I help you with something?"

Solana looked around for Maricella and saw her off in the distance, watering the vegetable garden, apparently unaffected by the strange men on her property. Maybe she knew the men, or they were there to help with something. Still, Solana stared at them suspiciously.

One of the men approached Ramón and held out a business card, while the other stood back, holding some wooden stakes and a large measuring tape.

"Didn't mean to startle you," the man said. "We just came by to do a little surveying."

"What for?" Solana stood beside Ramón.

"Solana, why don't you go inside?" Ramón suggested. He read

the card again and stuck it into his pocket. "Maybe you can start lunch—I'm starved."

"Forget it. I'm staying."

"We have permission to be here." The man handed another business card to Solana.

The words "Real Estate and Developing" jumped out at her. Doom enveloped her body.

"We're interested in buying the ranch," the man explained.

Solana handed the card back to him. "Sorry, it's not for sale."

"It is according to the owner." He gestured toward the garden. "His wife gave us the okay to start surveying. So if you don't mind . . ."

"Surveying what?" Solana trembled with anger and fear. Ramón put his hand on her arm. She yanked her arm away.

"Well, if we buy the land we plan to divide it into smaller lots. We just want to see what we have to work with."

Just like what Ellie was talking about. She pictured her uncle's ranch chopped into pieces. *So this was how Manuel planned to take care of things?* The man with the tape measure walked awkwardly away from the scene. He jammed one stake in the ground then ran his tape from the stake to a spot several feet away, where he stuck another one.

Solana took a step toward the man in front of her. "Well, you aren't dividing up *this* place."

"Solana," Ramón whispered. "I really think you should go in."

"If my uncle knew your plan, he wouldn't let you buy it," Solana almost yelled.

"He knows," the man said, "and he has no problem with it. Believe me, we are making it worth his while to sell. Now, why don't you take your friend's advice and go inside so we can finish our work."

Solana fought hard to keep her cool. But when she heard

another stake pierce the ground, something inside of her snapped. She charged toward the man doing the measuring. She yanked the stake up and threw it at his feet. "Leave!"

"Solana," Ramón said between his teeth.

From somewhere in the distance she heard her aunt yelling for her to stop.

"Ramón, tell them to leave." She looked helplessly at him, tears stinging her eyes.

Ramón shook his head. "This isn't up to me, Solana."

Maricella ran over, scolding Solana in Spanish and ordering her into the house.

"Uh, Jim." The man with the measuring tape leaned down slowly to retrieve the stake Solana had thrown. "I think we'd better come back another time."

"That's a good idea," Ramón said.

"You'd better not come back when I'm here," Solana shouted. She fought her aunt's grip on her arm.

"We'll call and make an appointment." The man with the stakes scowled at Solana.

Maricella shushed Solana and tried to nudge her toward the house but Solana stayed put. She could not take another step until she knew those men were gone. She watched every move they made until they were in their truck and driving away.

Before they were off the property, Maricella turned to her. "Solana, what is wrong with you?"

"What's wrong with *me*? How could you let them come here in the first place?"

Maricella took a deep breath. "We talked about it for a long time. It is better to sell than to let the loan company take our home."

"She has a point, Solana," Ramón said softly.

Solana whipped around to face him. "Did you know about this?"

"No." He looked at his shoes, then into her eyes. "It's their property, Sol. They know more about this than you do."

Tears choked Solana, making it impossible for her to say another word.

"Solana," Maricella said in a tight voice that sounded ready to break. "I appreciate all that you have done to help. But we must sell."

Solana shook her head. She pulled away from Maricella and headed toward the riding trails. Tears blurred her vision. "No," she moaned as her pace gradually built into a run. The farther she got from the ranch the more she felt it slipping from her grasp. Solana finally fell to her knees and sobbed.

"This can't be happening," she cried. "Please don't let this happen. Please." She covered her face.

Who am I even talking to? Am I going crazy?

She felt a hand on her shoulder and crumbled into deeper sobs.

"Solana," Ramón said. "Please calm down."

He sat beside her, his arm around her shoulders. At first he just sat with her, saying nothing. The only sound was Solana crying. She leaned into Ramón and rested her head against his chest, not caring if it was right or wrong.

"It's going to be okay," he whispered.

"How?" Solana's body heaved with sobs. Why did people always say "It's going to be okay," when they knew it wasn't true?

Ramón didn't answer.

"I tried so hard and it was all for nothing."

Ramón breathed in deeply. "I wish I knew what to say to make you feel better."

What could anyone say? Solana thought. Nothing. Nothing would make her feel better except to hear that the ranch was fine and Manuel didn't need to sell it.

When she ran out of tears, Solana stayed snuggled against

Ramón, enjoying the warmth of his arms. Even the silence felt comforting. Since the accident she'd spent every waking moment working, thinking, and planning. Now, she had no strength left.

Ramón squeezed her shoulder. "Feel better now?"

Solana sniffed. "I guess." She wiped her eyes and nose on her T-shirt.

"Sorry I didn't bring any tissue." Ramón guided Solana to sit up. "You know us dumb guys. We don't always think of things like that."

"That's okay." She looked up into his face. It was as kind and sweet as ever. "Us dumb girls don't always think of it either."

"Solana." Ramón sat back. "Please don't take this the wrong way, but I think it's time to give up. You've done everything you can."

"I don't want to give up." Solana rubbed her temples and thought. "But my brain's too tired to come up with anything else."

"Maybe you should stay away from this place for a few days." Ramón gazed into Solana's eyes. "You need a break."

Solana looked around. If Manuel was selling then she should spend as much time at the ranch as possible before it was gone. At the same time, how could she handle watching potential buyers tour the land? "I don't know," she said. "Maybe."

Without thinking about it she wrapped her arms around Ramón's neck. "Thanks."

"Sure," he whispered.

She held on to him for a minute then pulled away.

"I'm here any time you need me." He kissed her on the cheek.

Warm electricity lingered on Solana's cheek. They sat, just looking at each other. Memories of the many kisses that they'd shared on this same trail raced through Solana's mind, one by one. She leaned forward and kissed Ramón on the lips. He cupped her face with his hands and kissed her back.

chapter 17

Solana stared at the blank journal page, rolling the pen between her fingers. Her mind swam with the events of the day, replaying, again and again, the moment when she kissed Ramón. It felt so good to kiss him, even if the memory of it did feel kind of strange.

What were they supposed to do now? Act like that kiss never happened? Get back together? Even as they walked, hand in hand, back to the ranch, she had wondered. And something on Ramón's face had told her that he felt awkward too.

It would be great to have Ramón back. At least something good would come out of losing the ranch. She hung her head in her hands. *But he's leaving after the holidays.* She wished she were a year older so she could apply to MIT and go with him, even if it wasn't her college of choice. *This is crazy! We broke up for a good reason.*

She tossed her pen down and shoved her journal aside. How

could she think of her relationship with Ramón, with everything else going on?

A brochure from The Greenhouse lay on the desk, taunting her.

"That's right—I need to call Ellie," she whispered.

"Solana." Mamá knocked lightly on the bedroom door.

"Come in." Solana grabbed a magazine and pretended to read it. Solana didn't even need to ask what Mamá wanted. The "how-could-you-be-so-childish" look on her face said everything.

Mamá sat on Solana's bed.

"I know—Maricella called you," Solana said before her mother could speak.

"Solana, why would you embarrass her like that? She is going through enough."

Solana slouched in her chair. "I'm sorry, Mamá. I just snapped."

"Whatever Manuel and Maricella decide to do with the ranch is their business, not yours. You have gotten too involved."

Had she? Or was Mamá only saying that because Manuel and Maricella were upset? If they'd liked the idea of having the ranch protected, everyone would be praising her. "Solana is such a smart girl. We should have known she would come up with something."

Before Solana could defend herself, Mamá spoke up again. "Manuel is coming home tomorrow." She started to shake her finger at Solana then stopped and took a deep breath. "This is a very hard time for him and Maricella, Solana. Don't do anything else to upset them."

Solana's hands flew up in frustration but she kept her thoughts to herself. Why was Mamá acting like she'd been causing problems since day one?

Mamá stood. "If you go to the ranch to help, then *help*. They will need all they can get if they are going to get the place fixed up to sell, especially with Manuel off his feet."

Solana flipped the pages of the magazine in front of her. "Don't worry. I've run out of ideas anyway." She traced over a picture of a mountain lion with her finger. Her shoulders tightened. Did she even want to go to the ranch, knowing how Manuel felt about her actions?

Mamá walked over and wrapped her arms around Solana. She cradled her head and kissed it. "We will all miss the ranch, *mi'ja*."

Solana squeezed her eyes tight, not wanting to cry again. "I know. I keep forgetting I'm not the only one."

"But I know that next to Manuel and his family, you are more attached to it than anyone else is." Mamá patted her and let go. "I understand."

"Where are we going to have family reunions now? And parties?"

Mamá sighed. "We can have them here."

"It won't be the same."

"I know."

After Mamá left the room, Solana stood up, her eyes once again glued to The Greenhouse brochure. Ellie couldn't wait forever.

She reached for the cordless on her nightstand and sat on the edge of her bed. She methodically pushed numbers for The Greenhouse. After the last number she quickly pressed the "Off" button. *I can't do this yet.*

● ● ●

Solana sat between Becca and Tyler on one of the fallen logs in Alyeria. Jacie perched on the other side of Becca. Should she have chosen a place where Hannah could be included? *No.* She'd only talk about trusting God if she were here. Since they had allowed her into their secret place the one time to confront Tyler, Becca and Jacie had remained undecided about whether she should be invited on a regular basis.

"I've never felt so stuck." Solana watched a squirrel scamper across the ground. Her body slumped with exhaustion. "It's like, I think if I don't call Ellie then there's still hope—like my uncle can still change his mind. But waiting will only make me look like a flake. Plus I know my uncle *won't* change his mind—once it's set, it's set for good." She stomped her foot. "He's so stubborn!"

Becca and Tyler looked at each other and smirked.

"Yeah, I know," Solana said. "Like uncle, like niece." Once again tears sprang to her eyes. "I feel so let down. I really thought we had the answer."

"Me too," Becca said. "We prayed about it, and it seemed like everything was falling into place."

"Maybe God has another plan," Tyler suggested. "As frustrating as that sounds."

Solana watched the aspen leaves quake and shimmer in the gentle late-morning breeze. "Can you please not talk about God right now." The words just popped out. "He obviously isn't on my side."

"Okay, Sol." Tyler stroked Solana's back. He looked at Becca and Jacie. "We'll just listen."

"I'm afraid that Ellie will see me as a dumb kid who totally wasted her time."

Jacie leaned across Becca. "Ellie will understand, Solana. She's such a nice person. I'm sure this kind of thing happens all the time."

"You want us to go with you?" Tyler asked. "We promise to keep our mouths shut and let you do the talking."

Solana thought about it. It would be nice to have their support. But something inside her said differently. "I should probably be a big girl and go alone."

Tyler slapped his knees. "Well, if you change your mind . . ."

"I'll give you a call."

"We can wait in the car while you go in," Jacie offered.

"No." Solana sniffed hard. "I think I can handle it now. I guess

I just needed to see you guys before I went down there." She stood, then rolled her shoulders and swung her arms, like an athlete preparing for a big game. "I can do this," she whispered to herself. She sank back down onto the log. "What's wrong with me? Why am I acting like such a pathetic little wimp?"

Jacie moved from her spot and crouched in front of Solana. "You just aren't feeling very confident right now. It happens to all of us."

"Not to me. Not this bad."

"Well," Jacie said. "You've had a rough summer, Solana. You've had a rough year when you think about it."

Solana hung her head in her hands. "I've messed up a lot, you mean. I lost the district science fair so I probably won't get a scholarship to college. I blew it with Ramón. I lured Becca into that crazy Wicca group, so she almost sold her soul to the devil."

Becca laughed. "Don't exaggerate. It's not like you dragged me there kicking and screaming."

Tyler wrapped his arm around Solana and chuckled. "You're not the only one who's blown it recently. Think back to my antics in California."

"Well, my most recent antics affected my whole family."

"You did everything you could," Becca insisted.

"Then why do I feel like such a failure?" Solana looked up.

"Good question," Becca said. "Solana, think about it. You gave up half your summer working to save the ranch. You even gave up astronomy camp. I wouldn't have been that unselfish. And as far as the other stuff? You get straight A's in school and you've placed in every school science fair since I've known you. You are not a failure, no matter what happens with the ranch. You work too hard to ever call yourself that."

"You're just discouraged," Jacie said.

Solana felt a lump rise in her throat and swallowed it, tired of

dragonfly on my shoulder

137

crying. "That's an understatement."

Everyone fell silent. Before anyone had a chance to recommend a moment of prayer, Solana stood up. "I better get this over with."

As they ducked through the trees together, Solana wondered if she should have brought up her confusion over kissing Ramón. *Oh, why complicate things?* With her luck the kiss probably wouldn't even lead to anything worth getting her friends concerned about.

● ● ●

"Hi, Ellie." Solana stood just inside the doorway of the conservancy office, wishing that she'd called instead. Being there only reminded her of one more place that she'd never see again. Glancing around at the pictures, samples, and the diorama of Copper Ridge, it hit her how quickly she'd grown to love this cramped room with the fat cat and the earthy smells.

"Come on in." Ellie wiped her hands on a paper towel and ushered Solana inside. "I was just having a late lunch. Do you want some of this dried papaya? It's delicious." She held a plastic bag of fruit spears out to Solana. The sweet scent emanated from the top of the bag.

Solana shook her head. "No thanks." She sat stiffly in the chair beside Ellie's desk. Mr. P. rubbed his head against her leg and purred. She reached down to stroke him. "Did you dry the fruit yourself?"

"I wish." Ellie set the bag aside. "I'm not that much of an earth mother." She crossed her arms and leaned against a file cabinet. "So, did you talk to your uncle?"

Solana scratched under Mr. P.'s chin. Her heart ached. "Yes."

"And . . ." Ellie's voice was tender, like she knew exactly what Solana was about to say.

"He's not interested." Solana put her hands in her lap. Mr. P. looked up at her, waiting for more affection. She tried to explain her uncle's reservations. "He's selling the ranch." She almost told Ellie about the developers. But the idea of it was still too upsetting to even talk about. Though she hadn't planned on it, she found herself sharing how important the ranch was to her and her family. She even told Ellie about falling in love with Ramón there, skipping the part about when they had sex.

"No wonder you've fought so hard to keep it."

Solana nodded. On the drive over she'd come up with one last idea. She figured that she had nothing to lose by asking. "Is there any way *you* can talk to my uncle? Maybe if you explain how everything works . . ."

"Do you really think that would be a good idea, Solana?"

Solana shrugged. "It couldn't make things any worse."

"I have a feeling that in your uncle's case it's better not to push things any further. It sounds like he has his mind made up and I'm sure that choosing to sell was a very difficult decision for him."

Her last tiny bit of hope fizzled. "Well, I at least had to try."

"Of course you did. I would have done the same thing."

Ellie stepped away from the file cabinet. She rested her hand on Solana's back—a motherly touch that brought yet another lump to her throat. "I'm sorry this didn't work out."

Solana bit her lip to keep it from quivering. "I can't imagine not having the ranch. It's one of those things I assumed would always be there, you know—like family, or my friends." She surprised herself with her own openness. It was one thing to pour out her heart to Becca or Jacie, but to Ellie? She hardly knew the woman. At the same time she felt totally at ease, like she could tell Ellie anything.

"Those are the things that hurt the most to lose—the things we expect to have forever. But you know what I've learned? Nothing in this world is permanent." Ellie perched on the edge of her desk. She shook her head. "I'm sorry. I'm sure you don't want to hear something like that."

"It doesn't really help. But at least you didn't give me a sermon about this being God's will."

"No, that's not what you need either."

Solana swallowed hard. "Isn't that a Christian's job—to remind us sinners Who is in charge?"

"Not exactly."

"Sorry. I forget—my friends are used to my big mouth when it comes to God."

Ellie chuckled. She patted Solana's back. "Oh, nothing shocks me. My mouth used to be just as big as yours—still is sometimes. You're only being honest about how you feel." Ellie smiled. "Just don't let this get you too down, okay? It sounds like your uncle needs your support right now. You don't want to spend so much time getting in the way of his plans that you become part of the problem."

"That's the last thing I want to do." Solana looked up at Ellie's kind face. "Thanks for understanding—and for listening."

"Anytime. I mean that."

Looking around one last time, Solana got up. "I guess I'd better go. You probably have a lot of work to do."

"As always." Ellie reached out and gave Solana a hug. "Come by and visit sometime, okay?"

"Can I?" Solana returned Ellie's hug.

"Of course. Just because things didn't work out with your uncle doesn't mean you aren't welcome here."

Solana glanced at a pile of papers on Ellie's desk. "Maybe I can help you out sometime."

"I would love that."

"Then when I apply to Berkeley you can write me a glowing recommendation." Solana grinned.

"Hey, seeing you in action over the last week or so, I'd write you a recommendation based on that alone—you're definitely Berkeley material."

"Wow, thanks."

As Solana turned to leave the office, a weight seemed to lift from her shoulders.

chapter 18

When Solana returned home she pressed the "Message" button on the answering machine and flopped on the couch.

Beep

"Solana," Mamá's voice said. "I'm at the ranch helping Maricella with some things. Take some shredded pork out of the freezer, *por favor*, and I will make some tamales for dinner tonight. *Gracias*."

Beep

"Hey, Solana, it's Becca. I guess you're not back yet. Call me as soon as you get home! Jacie planned a girls-only night for tomorrow, so be at my house at six. No excuses! Oh, and it's a sleepover. Bye!"

Beep

"Solana, it's Ramón." Solana settled back on the couch, his voice soothing her spirits. "I just wanted to see how you are today. Give me a call, okay?"

"That is so like him," Solana said out loud. "Why did we have to mess things up so we couldn't be together?"

She reached for the cordless and dialed Ramón's number, the eagerness to talk to him building.

"Hello," Ramón's mother's recorded voice said. "You've reached 555–1642 . . ."

Great. What a day to play phone tag.

"Hey, Ramón." Solana's throat tightened. "It's Solana, returning your call." Keeping in mind that his mom might get the message before he did she cut it short. "I'll talk to you at the ranch later. Bye."

She pushed the "Off" button and let the tears stream down her cheeks.

● ● ●

"Pick a color." Becca held up two fistfuls of nail polish bottles.

Solana examined the rainbow of options. How could Becca hold 12 bottles at once? The cotton balls between her toes itched. She reached down to scratch her foot. "My brain is so fried right now. You know what I like, Becca. You pick before temporary insanity kicks in and I choose pink."

"No!" Becca gasped. "Not that! Not the pink polish." She clutched her chest, letting the bottles scatter across her lap.

Hannah wiggled her painted fingers. "Hey, pink is what I went with. It's really bright and fun. See?"

"Careful." Jacie caught Hannah's hand and set it down on the table. "You'll smear the polish."

Solana gave Hannah a weary smile. "What happened to the harlot red I suggested?"

"Not for my first manicure."

"That's right!" Jacie put down her polish. "This is a very special night—Hannah's first manicure."

Solana sighed dramatically. "Right up there with your first bra—I think I'm going to cry." She sniffed then whipped around to face Hannah. "Do your parents know what you're up to, young lady?"

Hannah laughed and rolled her eyes. "Yes—they're fine with it, as long as I don't start insisting on biweekly French manicures. They're not as archaic as you think, Solana."

"Well, we could debate for hours about that."

Becca quickly lined her bottles on the coffee table. "We must immortalize this moment." She hopped up from the couch, jogged to the table where Jacie and Hannah sat, and grabbed an emery board out of a packet. She presented it to Hannah, like a trophy. "Hannah Connor—some days come once in a lifetime."

"This is one of them." Jacie fought to keep her serious expression.

Becca placed the emery board in Hannah's outstretched hand. "May you never forget this important milestone."

Solana faced Hannah. "You're a woman now."

Hannah dabbed at her eyes. "I . . . I don't know what to say."

"Say that you'll let me paint each of your toes a different color." Jacie clasped her hands in expectation, mouthing "please, please."

Becca grabbed Hannah's arms. "Go for it, Hannah. Nobody will see it through your shoes. There's a whole world of polish out there, ripe for the taking."

Jacie leaned forward. "Colors like burgundy . . . lime green . . . neon blue."

Solana widened her eyes, picturing Hannah with multicolored toenails under her plain, sensible tennis shoes. "Jacie can even add some funky designs, like polka dots, and stars and stripes."

Hannah gazed at the ceiling, resting a finger under her chin, pondering the possibilities. Finally she decided. Her eyes twinkled. "Okay. Let's do it."

Jacie clapped her hands. "I've been dying to do this!"

"And I will always treasure this." Hannah held up the emery board.

Becca made her way back to the couch.

"You be careful with that thing, Hannah," Solana shook her finger at Hannah. She swung her feet back onto the couch. "Emery boards may look harmless but they can be deadly weapons."

Hannah stuck her gift in her pocket. "I'll keep it in a safe place, out of the reach of my younger siblings."

Becca flopped back down and took Solana's foot in her lap. Solana slapped her leg. "Give me the brightest shade of purple you have in this place."

Solana relaxed as Becca shook a bottle of Ultra-Violet polish and began painting her toenails. "Thanks for thinking this up, Jace."

"You're welcome." Jacie examined Hannah's nails. "Becca's mom stocked the fridge with ice cream and rented two movies for us. We're set for the night."

"I should have brought some of the candy I got today," Hannah said.

"That's right!" Jacie almost dropped her polish. "Hannah, tell Solana about that. She'll love it!"

Solana turned her neck to see Hannah and Jacie. "What will I love?"

Jacie grinned. "Hannah's secret admirer strikes again."

"You mean the rose guy from the ski trip?"

Hannah blushed. "Yes. I met Jacie at Copperchino during her lunch today. I had my mom's car because I was running an errand for her. Well, when I left the coffeehouse there was a box on my car full of Twix candy bars, and a gift certificate to Copperchino."

Becca stuck her polish brush back into the bottle. "Who *is* this guy?"

Hannah shook her head. "I have no idea."

Solana turned back around. "I bet Tyler's the guy."

"No." Hannah shook her head. "On the ski trip he insisted it wasn't him."

"But whoever it is knows that Twix is your favorite candy bar," Jacie pointed out.

"And that you go to the Copperchino," Becca added. "So it's someone who knows you."

Hannah shrugged. "I can't think of anyone."

Solana tried to imagine Hannah's super-conservative parents reacting to their daughter's secret admirer. "I'm surprised your parents let you out of the house tonight, knowing that there's a guy out there—*liking you*."

She and Becca looked at each other with wide eyes and open mouths. "Ooo!"

Hannah swiveled around. "I didn't tell them—not yet anyway."

Jacie grabbed Hannah's hand again. "Quit moving. I'm almost done."

"Sorry."

"Wow," Becca said. "It has been a long time since we did something like this—just hanging out and having fun together."

"Yeah." Solana's mood threatened to take a melancholy turn. "We've spent every moment at the ranch. You guys haven't had any time for fun."

Becca blew on Solana's toenails then started on the other foot. "Who says we didn't have fun?"

"We loved it," Hannah said.

"What do you mean?" Solana tried to think. *Didn't they see all their work as a waste of time?* Some days even she felt that way. "You spent half your summer working for something that flopped in the end. Your prayers weren't answered. Doesn't that make you mad at all?"

"It doesn't seem like they were," Hannah said. "But God doesn't always answer prayer the way we want Him to—He answers in the way we need."

Jacie twisted her polish bottle shut. "Of course, that's easy for us to say. We're not the ones losing something valuable to us."

Hannah corrected herself. "I'm not saying we aren't disappointed for you, Solana—we are."

Solana's heart felt like it was being dragged down to her stomach. "Let's not talk about this tonight, okay? I want to forget real life for a while." She decided to finally tell her friends about her tattoo. If that wouldn't get the conversation moving in a new direction, nothing would.

Becca ran her thumb around the outside of Solana's baby toe, catching a drip. "Yeah, this is supposed to be a fun night."

Solana pretended to scratch an itch on her shoulder. How should she bring it up?

Jacie picked up a file and halfheartedly ran it over her thumbnail, her eyes lost in thought. Suddenly she giggled. "We should play one of those silly slumber party games later—like Truth or Dare."

Becca's face lit up. "Yeah."

Solana put her hand down, sensing that her big announcement was once again on hold.

Hannah looked from Jacie to Solana. "I've never played that."

"You haven't?" Jacie slammed her fist on the table. "It's settled then. We have to play. Oh, let's do it now! Your toes can wait until later."

"Solana's too." Becca twisted the top back onto the violet polish and plunked it on the table. "Who's first?" She turned to Solana, crisscrossing her legs on the couch. "Solana!"

"Why me?"

"Because you'll show Hannah what the game's all about. So, which is it? Truth or dare?"

"Truth," Solana blurted out. She glanced at each of her friends. She straightened her shoulders and flipped her hair. "I have nothing to hide."

"Okay." Becca leaned her chin in her hand. Her head shot up. "How old were you the first time you kissed a boy?"

Solana raised her eyebrows, thinking back—way back. *How did Becca not know this information? And why did so many questions directed at her have to be about boys? Oh, why ruin a fun night trying to analyze a dumb question?*

"Kindergarten." She smirked, remembering the incident. Jake Robinson was the cutest boy in rooms K–1 and K–2 combined. "I got in so much trouble." Solana covered her face.

"For kissing a boy at school?" Hannah giggled. "Was it against the rules?"

"I got in trouble for chasing Jake into the boys' bathroom to kiss him."

Becca almost fell off the couch laughing. "That is so like you, Solana!"

That's me, Solana thought. *Who am I if not Solana the Boy-Crazy?* She took a deep breath to chase away the strange unexplainable feeling rising inside her. But she wanted to feel like her old boy-crazy self. Wasn't that her original motivation for getting a tattoo—before it became a ranch memento?

"My turn." Solana scanned the room. Who to pick next? She chuckled wickedly when she finally decided. "Hannah. Truth or dare?"

Hannah bit her lip. She smiled as she looked at Jacie and Becca for guidance—or maybe protection. Both girls shook their heads as if to say, "You're on your own." Finally Hannah turned to Solana. "Dare."

"Oh!" Jacie and Becca shouted together.

Solana rubbed her palms together. "This is going to be fun."

"Be nice," Jacie whispered. "It's her first time playing."

Solana licked her lips and grinned, thinking hard. *Be nice? No way—Truth or Dare was not about being nice.* "Okay, got it." She jumped up and grabbed the phone. "You call Tyler and pretend to be Jessica. When he answers you say . . ."

Hannah shook her head. "No. I won't lie. That's where I draw the line."

Solana sank back on the couch. "I should have known." She went back to thinking. Again, she hopped up. This time she searched a nearby drawer for paper and a pen.

"What are you doing?" Becca craned her neck to watch Solana.

Solana returned to the couch and started scribbling on the pad of paper. "Tonight Hannah makes her first prank phone call."

Hannah turned beet-red. "I can't do something like that."

"You can and you will," Solana scolded.

Jacie and Becca watched over Solana's shoulder as she wrote Hannah's script. Her friends were right. It was doing her good to forget her family problems and have some girls-only fun.

"Solana, that prank call is so old." Jacie tapped the page with her finger.

Solana slapped her hand away. "You're in my light."

Becca shook her head. "I did that one in third grade. You could at least pick something new."

Solana scowled playfully at Becca and Jacie. "I could make her say something obscene. I'm being nice, like you said."

Hannah tried to peek at Solana's paper. Solana pulled the pad to her chest. "Back, woman." After adding one last sentence she handed the script to Hannah. "After you dial the phone number you have to read this word for word. And no laughing or saying, 'Oh, I can't do this.' You picked dare, baby. There's no turning back."

Becca ran for the phone book. She flipped to a page, pointed to a number, and read it to Hannah.

Hannah took several deep breaths before dialing. Jacie perched on the edge of her chair, already choking back laughter. "I can't believe we're doing this. How old are we again?"

"Sh!" Solana held up her hands, silencing the group. They all sat, awestruck, as Hannah slowly dialed.

Becca scurried to the telephone cradle and pressed the button for speaker-phone, so everyone could hear.

"Hello," an elderly sounding woman said.

"Hello, ma'am, is this Mrs. Wall?" Hannah's eyes widened with terror.

"No, it is not. You have the wrong number, honey."

Hannah glanced at Solana, who pointed to the paper.

"Well, is Mr. Wall there?"

"No, dear, I'm sorry. There are no Walls here."

Jacie and Becca doubled over, releasing squeaks of repressed laughter. Solana sat spellbound, wishing Tyler could witness such a moment.

Hannah couldn't keep the smile off of her face. "Well, if there are no walls, then what's holding up your house?" She covered her mouth before a laugh escaped.

"Young lady," the woman snapped. "Don't you have anything better to do with your time than to . . ."

"Quick, hang up!" Solana grabbed the phone from Hannah and pressed "Off."

Hannah and Solana joined Becca's and Jacie's screams of laughter.

"I can't believe that I just did that." Hannah wiped tears from her eyes.

"I wouldn't mention this when you apply to Bible college if I were you." Solana's stomach and face muscles ached from holding back for so long. She looked at Hannah, whose cheeks hadn't lost their red tinge. "Oh man!" She howled. "I definitely needed this!"

chapter 19

"Becca," Solana whispered. "Are you awake?"

"Yeah."

Jacie and Hannah breathed low and even, telling Solana that they were out cold. Solana unzipped her sleeping bag a little and rested her elbow on the pillow, to prop herself up. Becca turned over in her bed.

"What's up?" Becca rolled out of bed and sat on the floor.

As soon as she and her friends had settled into their sleeping bags in Becca's room, the lights went out, and things got quiet, Ramón had invaded Solana's mind and refused to leave. Somehow she knew she was in for a sleepless night unless she got her thoughts out of her head. Becca would probably give her the lecture of a lifetime when she heard about the big kiss with Ramón, but she didn't care. Maybe the fear of waking up Jacie and Hannah would keep Becca from going off too much.

"Something happened with Ramón the other day."

"What?" Becca pulled her pillow off the bed and stretched out on the floor. "Are you okay?"

"I guess."

Becca's eyes overflowed with such concern and caring that Solana had to avoid looking into them. "I'm just more confused than ever."

"Does he have another girlfriend or something?"

"No." She considered the possibility. "Maybe it would make things easier if he did. At least I'd know, once and for all, where we stood with each other." Then again, the idea of Ramón kissing another girl . . .

Careful to keep her voice down, Solana told Becca her biggest secret—that she'd kissed Ramón.

"It's like, I want to get back together with him. But then again, what's the point if he's leaving in a few months?"

"Solana, you kissed him because you were upset—one of those heat-of-the-moment things. It's not a reason to get back together."

Solana lay back on her pillow and stared at the ceiling. "I can't stop thinking about him and wanting to be with him."

"But Solana, look how long it took for you to get over Ramón. Do you really want to have everything start over? Can you be with him without . . . you know . . . *being* with him?"

How many times had she tossed that question around in her head, weighing what she wanted to be true against reality? "I know I hate being without him. Maybe getting Ramón back will be the one good thing that comes out of this whole mess with the ranch."

"Or maybe there's some other good thing. Ellie is writing you a recommendation to UC Berkeley. That's something great right there." Becca lay back too. "I just don't want to see you get hurt again, Solana. I think it has been good for you to be without a guy for a while."

Solana glanced at Becca out of the corner of her eye. How could she say such a thing? Didn't she see how out of control Solana felt? "But I'll never find another one as perfect as Ramón, so maybe I should stick with him."

"Or maybe you should just start being more picky. Ramón showed you what you are looking for. So why waste time dating jerks? Put your energy into more important things, like Hannah said."

"Like what?"

"Like college, and all the amazing scientific discoveries that you have planned." Becca propped herself up with her elbow. "You don't need to have a guy in your life to feel valuable, you know. I know it makes you feel good about yourself to have guys drooling over you. But you are worth more than that, Solana, and you know it. I know that the whole Ramón thing changed you forever. But you know what? I think you are better for it, in a way. When you stopped dating every cute guy that you saw, you started to become your own person. You just don't see it because you aren't on the outside watching."

How had this turned into a conversation about Solana and how she felt about herself?

"Just take some time to think, okay, Solana? Even if you need to stay away from the ranch so you won't be tempted by Ramón's presence so much."

"You're not the first person to suggest that I stay away. My family thinks I've gotten too involved and need to let *Tío* Manuel make his own decisions."

"Maybe they're right. As much as it hurts, I think it's time to let Ramón and the ranch go."

"I just wish I knew how."

● ● ●

Three days away from the ranch was all Solana could handle. The longer she avoided Manuel, the more she dreaded the day when she'd have to face him. Ramón called twice, saying he missed her—making it even harder to take Becca's advice.

"I miss you, too," she said during both calls. Becca's warnings played like an annoying song she couldn't get out of her head.

A large "For Sale" sign greeted her as she drove onto her uncle's property. So it really was official. The finality of it all gripped her. Did the sign mean the developers had decided against the land?

She fixed her eyes on a pair of Manuel's horses grazing in the field. The thought of those horses being divided up like a bunch of orphaned children was more than she could handle.

She hesitated before knocking on the door of the house. Solana knocked lightly, still thinking of what she might say to her aunt and uncle.

Maricella welcomed Solana with a warm smile. "You don't have to knock, Solana."

Solana gripped her purse strap. "Well, I figured after the other day, I should." She straightened her shoulders. *Toughen up, girl. Quit acting like a scared little kid. This is your family.* She took a deep breath. "Maricella, I'm sorry about throwing a fit when those guys were here. That was so immature."

Maricella led Solana to the couch. "You were upset. We all were."

"I just wanted you guys to keep this place so badly. I still want that."

Maricella nodded. A cloud of sadness filled her eyes. "Yes, I know." She patted Solana's leg. "You are forgiven."

"Thanks." Solana looked around for signs of her uncle. A wheelchair sat folded in the corner of the living room. "Um. Is *Tio* Manuel around?"

Maricella rose and headed for the back porch. "Manuel," she called, "someone is here for you."

They found Manuel out back, tightening a screw on a patio chair. One of his legs was still in a cast and a cane rested against the picnic table.

"What is this?" Maricella put her hands on her hips.

Manuel stopped, like a little boy caught with his hand in the cookie jar. He sat back stiffly, cringing as he straightened his back. "The legs on this chair are wobbly. You have been nagging me to fix it for a long time."

"That was before the accident." Maricella sighed for effect. She picked up the chair and set it down hard. "The doctor said too much bending will hurt your back. And what do you do? Bend over to fix a chair."

Manuel dropped his screwdriver on the table. "Would it be better if I sit in this broken chair and it collapses under me?"

Maricella picked up the screwdriver. "If it is broken, we will put it in the shed. We have plenty of others." She nodded toward Solana. "Besides, you have a visitor." Before heading down the steps toward the shed she whispered to Solana, "Do not let him out of your sight. He thinks he is still 18 years old and can work no matter what."

Solana laughed in spite of her nervousness, watching her pouting uncle. But as soon as Maricella left the two of them alone, her insides tightened again. She sat across from Manuel at the picnic table.

"Hey." She willed her shoulders to relax. "Is it good to be home?"

Manuel looked around, his eyes full of frustration. "When I am not being treated like a *bebe*."

"She's only trying to help you get better."

"All my life I have worked—sick or healthy." Manuel looked at the ground. He tapped his toe, making the silence even more awkward.

"*Tío* Manuel, I'm really sorry. I . . ."

He reached for Solana's hand and squeezed it. "You were trying to help me. I would have done the same thing for your *familia*." He let go of her hand and stood up slowly, looking past the porch toward his stable. "It just killed me the whole time I was in the hospital, knowing time was ticking away and there was nothing I could do. The day you came to see me I had just given the okay to sell. Maybe that is why I blew up like I did. It's not that your idea was so bad." Manuel shook his head.

"No, I should have run it by you first." Solana got up and stood beside her uncle. "Are you still selling?"

Manuel nodded. "Maybe it is for the best." Manuel tapped his cane on the ground. "As much as I don't like to say it—my body is taking longer to heal than I planned. And it will only get harder when Ramón goes away to school. I guess Maricella is right—I am getting old."

"You are not." Solana gave her uncle a half-hug. "But who knows. Maybe this is the beginning of something new for you and *Tía* Maricella." She wasn't sure who she was trying harder to convince—her uncle or herself.

Manuel smiled down at her. "Maybe."

She tried to put herself in his place, but that place hurt too much. She thought she was losing everything, while her aunt and uncle were losing a hundred times more. She was losing her favorite place—they were losing their home.

● ● ●

"So, do you feel better after talking to your uncle?" Ramón leaned against the stall.

Solana let out a deep sigh. "Yes." She looked around the inside of the stable. Would whoever bought the ranch change things around or leave them the same? They'd better leave them the same. "I still have a hard time dealing with the fact that this place will be sold soon."

Ramón brushed some dirt off his shirt. "The only people who've checked the place out are the developers you chased off. They haven't called since."

Solana looked up at Ramón innocently. "I hope I didn't scare them away."

"Apparently one of the men is still having nightmares about you."

Solana swatted Ramón's arm playfully. "Good! I hope he spreads rumors about me all over the real estate industry so nobody wants to buy the place."

Ramón laughed. "That wouldn't be good for your uncle though. He really needs to sell soon or he and your aunt will run out of money."

"I know." Solana folded her arms. "At least he plans to stay in Copper Ridge." She leaned against the stall, next to Ramón. "So, I bet you'll be looking for a job somewhere else pretty soon—at least until you leave for MIT."

"I'll stick around here until Manuel sells. It'll be tough to find a job as good as this one."

"I bet."

"At first it was hard because . . . well . . . you were here so much, too. Then after the accident I could tell you were hurting, and I wanted to be there for you but didn't know how close I should get."

Solana stayed quiet and listened.

"But the more you were around, the closer I wanted to get." Ramón looked into Solana's eyes. "The other day, when we kissed—well, I've been thinking about it ever since. It was like things were back to the way they used to be."

Solana smiled, remembering it. "I know."

"Since then I've been thinking maybe we can try going out again. Do you want to go to a movie or something?"

"I want to." Solana looked at the ground for a moment, then back at Ramón. "But Ramón, what then? I mean, we can't be together like we were before, but we can't start over either."

"Why not? We've given each other some time, and it's obvious we still love each other. We can do things differently this time."

Can we really? Is that actually possible? Looking into Ramón's tender eyes, she wanted with all her heart to make it possible. "But you're going away to school."

"I've been thinking about that, too." Ramón reached out and stroked Solana's hair. "I don't want to tie you down once I'm gone. At the same time, I know I'll always love you."

Solana smiled coyly. "Yeah, I know. I have so many irresistible qualities."

"Be serious."

"I am serious." She worked hard to put on a serious expression. The moment seemed too intense to handle without breaking it up with smart remarks. It was either laugh or cry, and she'd done enough crying already. "I'll always love you, too."

"So why can't we spend time together? I mean, I know we took things way too fast before. I also know it's unrealistic to talk about being exclusive when we'll be so far away from each other. But I don't want anyone but you."

"Me neither." Solana smiled, feeling her eyes moistening.

Ramón grabbed Solana's hands. "We obviously can't date while I'm off at school. In a year you'll be in college too. We both have major goals to focus on. So, we have no choice but to take things slow. Let's try going to a movie once in a while. Or we can do things with your friends."

Solana finished his thought. "So we won't be alone together."

"Right." Ramón squeezed her hands and laughed. "For now—because I can't control myself when I'm alone with you. But being away from you is even worse."

Solana wrapped her arms around Ramón's neck. "I'm going to miss you so much when you leave."

"I'll miss you, too," he whispered into her hair. "But at least we know things haven't ended for us."

Solana nodded, letting Ramón's embrace envelop her, melting away her doubts and fears.

chapter 20

Solana pulled a black blouse off the clearance rack and held it up. Under the lights of the outlet store, the fabric had a hint of shimmer.

"That's cute." Jacie ran her fingers over the material. She looked at the price tag. "Get it. At Raggs By Razz we sell those tops for three times as much."

"I'm sold." Solana added the blouse to the pile hanging over her arm. After all that had happened over the summer, it felt weird to be doing something as normal as back-to-school shopping.

"I can't believe that it's time for school to start already." Hannah perused a rack of half-priced skirts.

Becca joined her, checking out some jeans that were on the same rack. "And this year we rule the school!"

Hannah held up a denim skirt then quickly put it back on the rack.

Solana rushed over. "Hey, what are you doing? That'll look good on you." She retrieved the skirt and held it up to Hannah. "It's perfect. Try it on."

Hannah shook her head. "It's nice, but it looks kind of tight."

Solana snorted. "Tight? You obviously haven't seen half of my wardrobe. This is *not* tight—it's straight—sleek. And it's long so you don't have to worry about being revealing." She shook the skirt, waiting for Hannah to accept it. "You can get away with this style, unlike some of us. You have a perfect body. At least try it."

Hannah hesitated. She took the skirt and studied it more closely. "It is nice." She giggled, like she was about to try on a slinky negligee. "Okay, I'll try it on."

"Good girl." Solana walked beside Hannah as the group made their way toward the dressing rooms. "For your senior year you cannot show up at school dressed like a nun."

Hannah raised her armload of clothing choices. "Do you see any nun clothes here?"

Jacie and Becca ran ahead to get a spot in the long line that had formed outside the dressing rooms.

Solana lifted a few of the items. Hannah's pile consisted mostly of dresses and long skirts, but she'd managed to find a couple of cute tops to try on—a big step for Hannah. "I guess you're learning."

Hannah hugged her pile of clothes. "You know, Solana, this is really fun. It's my first back-to-school shopping trip, you know."

Solana checked the price on a pair of jeans. "We'll have to get you an ice cream later, to celebrate."

Hannah grinned. "It's nice to see you back to your old self—actually, a better version of yourself."

Solana raised her eyebrows. "Is that a compliment?"

"Of course! I don't know how to explain what I mean, but it's like all that you've gone through has brought out a good side of you—a more mature side."

"Thanks." *Wow, two comments like that in a week.* Solana returned Hannah's smile. "It's brought out a good side of you, too. I never knew you were such a good rancher. Have you considered doing it for a living?"

Hannah shook her head and groaned. "Like I said, you're back to your old self."

They caught up with Jacie and Becca.

"This line is so long." Becca leaned against the wall. She put one foot against the wall, until a sales lady walked by and gave her a dirty look.

Jacie stood on her tiptoes to see over the sea of heads. "That's what we get for waiting until the week before school starts."

"So," Becca said. "While we're waiting, let's make a plan for this Friday night. How about swimming and pizza at my house?"

Hannah stopped to think. "I can probably make it."

"Me too," Jacie said. "I get off work at six that night."

Solana hesitated before giving Becca an answer. She and Ramón had talked the day before about doing something over the weekend but were still undecided about a plan. *I can't believe I'm suggesting this, but here goes.* She cleared her throat. "So Becca, what would you think if I brought a friend along on Friday?"

"Who? Kara?"

"No—Ramón."

Becca, Jacie, and Hannah looked at each other.

"We're not back together exclusively right now. We had a talk and we're taking things slow. He mentioned doing stuff with you guys once in a while."

Becca nodded after a moment. "No, no—bring him. I think it's a good thing. Nothing could possibly happen if you're with us."

Becca smiled coyly. "I invited Nate, too. Nate, Ramón, and Tyler can do some male bonding."

Jacie nudged Hannah. "One of these days maybe you'll bring Mystery Guy to one of our Friday night get-togethers."

"That is, if I ever find out who he is—and if I can sell him on the courtship idea."

"Ha!" Solana huffed. "Good luck."

Before they knew it, the line had moved ahead and Jacie was next up. The woman manning the dressing rooms handed her a tiny plastic hanger and pointed toward a room.

"That room's pretty large if you girls want to double up and make the line go faster," the woman suggested.

Jacie looked at Hannah. "You want to go in with me?"

Hannah shook her head, blushing a little. "I'll wait."

Solana was about to jump at the chance. Then she remembered the tattoo that she still hadn't shown her friends. A public dressing room wasn't her idea of a good place for the big unveiling. She turned to Becca. "Go ahead."

"Okay." Becca followed Jacie.

While Solana waited, she leaned against the wall. *When should I show them the tattoo? Since I've waited this long I might as well make it good.*

● ● ●

"Wear that denim skirt on the first day of school," Solana instructed Hannah. She opened Jacie's car door. "I have the perfect top to go with it."

"Great," Hannah teased. "Then my mom won't let me out of the house."

"What? She has something against leopard print?"

"Hey," Becca interrupted. "What's your uncle doing here?"

Solana shut the car door, spotting the familiar car in her parents' driveway. "Maybe he's here for dinner or something. I should get inside." Suddenly her heart dropped. "I hope he didn't come over to announce that he found a buyer. I'm not ready for that yet."

"Oh, let's hope not," Becca said.

"Call us later," Jacie said. "We want to know what's going on."

Hannah leaned out the window. "All of us."

"I will." Solana took her time walking toward the house.

chapter 21

"Hi, Becca." Solana fought hard to keep emotion out of her voice.

"Is everything okay? I've been going crazy since we dropped you off."

"I need to talk to all of you. Meet me at Alyeria, okay?"

"What about Hannah?"

Solana thought. Of course she wanted to tell Hannah—she'd been in on everything all summer long. But would Jacie and Tyler mind if she let Hannah in on an Alyeria meeting without talking to the whole group first? *I don't have time for a big group discussion.*

"Invite Hannah, too—this time. Tell Jacie and Tyler this is important. I'm sure they'll understand."

"Okay, but—are you all right?"

"Just meet me."

● ● ●

Solana paced back and forth in the old aspen grove. She sat on a log, then hopped up again. What was keeping everyone?

"I hope she's okay." She heard Hannah in the distance. "How did she sound on the phone?"

"I couldn't tell," Becca said. "She was like, emotionless."

"She must be really upset then." Jacie's concern came through in her voice.

"Poor Solana," Tyler said.

"If you're so worried about poor Solana," Solana yelled, "then get in here so she can spill her guts and you can support her like good friends are supposed to."

They entered the grove one by one, all looking like they didn't know whether to worry or strangle Solana. As soon as they were all inside she smiled. She squealed and ran over to hug each of them individually.

"Have you completely lost it?" Tyler pulled away from Solana's hug.

"What's going on?" Becca sat on a log.

Solana sat beside Becca and waved for everyone to gather around. "Since so many of our Alyeria meetings happen because one of us is having a problem, I thought I'd use this place to share something exciting."

"What?" Jacie's eyes widened with anticipation.

Enjoying the suspense on her friends' faces Solana let them sit for a minute, staring at them all, before Becca finally cracked.

"No more games! Tell us what's going on."

"Okay, okay, I can't stand keeping this inside anymore anyway." She started bouncing up and down, feeling silly, but unable to contain her excitement. "Manuel is selling the ranch!"

"What?!" everyone said at once. They looked at each other, then at Solana.

Jacie shook her head. "But you're happy."

"Because he won't have to move." She smiled thinking about it. "He's selling it to The Greenhouse."

Hannah raised her arms then let them drop again. "But I thought . . ."

"He changed his mind. You guys, he *never* does that." Solana shook her head. "When I first saw my uncle's face today, I was like, great, what did I do now? Then he started smiling at me. I could have smacked him for giving me a heart attack like that."

"What changed his mind?" Tyler asked.

"The developers called the other day, ready to offer him a deal. Manuel just couldn't do it. It hit him—if the developers divided his ranch into smaller ranchettes, everything he had worked for would be destroyed. They would demolish his fields, the pasture, whatever was in their way. So he said, 'No thanks.' But nobody else has shown interest in the ranch, so he was a little freaked out about the future."

Solana stopped for a breath. "Later he came across Ellie's card and decided he didn't have anything to lose by asking a few questions. He and my aunt talked to her, and they came up with a plan—they're selling half of the land to Ellie. It turns out the ranch is made up of two lots. One has the house, stable, and fields. The other lot is basically Dragonfly Pond, the pasture, and trails. He bought it so the horses would have a place to graze and so he'd never have to worry about anyone building too close to his property." She shook her head, the wonderful shock of it all still sinking in. "I always thought the ranch was one huge piece of land."

"So he's selling the lot with Dragonfly Pond on it?" Tyler asked.

"Right. The money he gets from the sale will help him keep up his loan payment on the house."

Becca raised her fists in triumph. "So is it all official?"

"Not yet. But Ellie has already tested the pond for that fungus she was worried about—it's called chytrid, and it kills boreal toads.

Anyway, the pond doesn't have any."

"What about restrictions?" Hannah asked.

"Manuel will be caretaker of the land The Greenhouse owns," Solana explained. "As long as there is someone willing to care for the land, caretakership will be passed down in his family. The only restrictions are that he keep the land in its natural state and keep growing hay, since it benefits wetlands."

"Oh, Solana," Jacie said. "That's wonderful."

They all tried to hug her at once.

"See," Becca said, still holding on to Solana, "we should never give up."

"Actually," Tyler chuckled, "everything fell into place when we did give up."

"Yeah." Solana sat back. "I don't get that."

Hannah crossed her arms. "And I never thought to pray for Manuel to have a change of heart."

Jacie shrugged, smiling. "Maybe God didn't give you the idea because it was *His* idea and He wanted us to enjoy the surprise of seeing Him work in a way we wouldn't expect."

"Well, I'd pretty much given up on the idea of Him wanting to help. He sure blew me away." Solana's last phrase flew out before she could pull the words back. When four faces turned her way, all wearing the same hopeful expression, she tried to cover up her statement. "I mean . . ."

"It's okay to give Him the credit," Hannah said. "Who else are you going to give it to? This is a miracle that could have come only from God."

"Well, I don't care how it happened," Solana said. "I'm just glad it did."

chapter 22

Manuel and Maricella's ranch buzzed with the voices of relatives, friends, and Solana's friends' families, who'd come to celebrate Manuel's recovery. Stereo speakers had been moved outside so that everyone could hear Manuel's favorite Spanish guitar CDs. Intricately designed *luminarias* lit up the porch rail and picnic tables.

"This thing is rigged!" Becca tore off the blindfold and tossed the baseball bat to Ramón.

Ramón caught the bat in midair. "Tell me, Becca, how does one rig a *piñata?*"

Becca walked in a slow circle around the giant rocket-shaped *piñata* dangling from the branch of an old oak tree behind Manuel's house, examining it from every angle. "You had it made extra thick or something."

"Yeah, that's it."

Solana took the bat from Ramón. "Becca just can't handle defeat." She handed the bat to Alvaro and ordered Becca to tie the blindfold on him.

Ellie watched from the porch, swaying gently to the music as she munched on a small bowl of chips and salsa. She smiled at Solana.

"Hey, Ellie." Solana waved back. "I'm glad you could make it." Actually, it felt a little strange to have Ellie at a family gathering. But everyone had agreed she should meet the relatives, now that her conservancy would soon own part of the ranch.

An unexpected melancholy came over Solana as she watched Ellie stroll over and mingle with her cousins. Soon *she* would control part of the ranch instead of *Tío* Manuel.

All week long, through the chaos and excitement of the first week of senior year, Solana, overcome by relief, had been walking with her feet barely touching the ground. Finally, after so much hard work, they knew for sure that Manuel would not lose his ranch. But it had come at a price—Dragonfly Pond, the riding trails, and much of the open pasture. That price suddenly hurt.

She studied her uncle, who was leaning on his cane while he talked to her father. No wonder Manuel had been so quiet since making his decision to sell to The Greenhouse. A part of her wanted to sit down and be quiet too. The family would always care for and use the protected land, but soon it would no longer belong to them. For the first time she understood Manuel's reservations when he first heard her idea.

But he kept his home, so it's worth it.

A crack of the bat brought Solana back to the party.

"Whoa, Alvaro!" Becca shouted.

Hannah clapped her hands. "He's stronger than you, Becca."

Becca put her hands on her hips. "Way to make me look bad, little man."

Jacie squealed. "That was awesome! Did you see that hit, Solana? Becca, your parents should sign him up for tee-ball."

Everyone cheered and laughed as Alvaro stood under a downpour of candy and small toys that fell over his dark hair. "I did it." Realizing the treasure that lay at his feet, Alvaro fell to his knees and began stuffing candy into the pockets of his shorts.

"Slow down, buddy." Becca pulled Alvaro back. "Save some for the other kids."

"Yeah, like me." Tyler pushed his way between Jacie and Becca and dove for the candy heap.

Hannah laughed. "Tyler, that's for the children."

Tyler jumped up and handed Hannah a red lollipop and a plastic kazoo. "Here. You know you want some."

The CD changed to a bittersweet Spanish melody—one that matched Solana's mood a little too well. She leaned down and snatched a piece of bubble gum before one of the kids could grab it. She unwrapped the pink chunk and popped it into her mouth. "Come on." She tugged on Jacie's arm. "Let's take a walk to the pond."

● ● ●

Solana stretched out on the ground with Jacie, who laughed at Becca, Hannah, and Tyler trying to catch dragonflies with their hands. Her heart pulled into a tighter knot. She blew a gigantic bubble. It popped with a loud smack. *It's not like I can't come here anymore.*

Hannah sank breathlessly beside Jacie. "It's hard to believe the last time we were here things looked completely hopeless."

Solana leaned back on her elbows, fighting against the sadness. "Yeah."

"I noticed that Elijo showed up today." Tyler made one more grab for a dragonfly then gave up. "That's a first."

Solana rolled her eyes. "He may miss a family emergency, but he never misses a party."

Jacie cocked her head to one side and gazed tenderly into Solana's eyes. "Hey, Sol, what's wrong? You look sad."

"I know I shouldn't be, but I am a little." She let her feelings about selling Dragonfly Pond pour out.

Becca and Tyler joined Solana, Jacie, and Hannah on the ground. Nobody seemed to know what to say.

Solana picked a blade of grass and rolled it between her fingers. "I never really thought about how this would feel."

Becca moved closer to Solana. "Solana, this is what we wanted."

"I know." Solana chuckled, realizing how silly she sounded. She'd gotten her way and now all she could do was complain and feel sad. "I guess the whole idea just sank in—that it won't be the same."

"This is God's best for your family," Hannah said. "So everything is going to be okay."

"Oh, I don't know what's wrong with me." Solana stood up and straightened her dress. "Things are falling into place so quickly. Maybe that's why this feels weird—it's happening so fast. Even Ellie is surprised. She's just waiting on some grant money before she starts the official paperwork. I guess money is an ongoing problem with conservancies. And people aren't as generous with donations these days."

"God will provide." Hannah patted Solana's shoulder.

Solana folded her arms. "Did He just send you a direct message from above or something?"

"No, I just have confidence that if He worked things out to this point, He's not going to drop the ball in the last stage."

Tyler hopped up. "Oh, and guess what—my mom wants to do a story for *Brio* about us working all summer to save this place. She thought it might encourage teenagers to think about how they can meet the needs of others. She's going to mention The Greenhouse. So, who knows, maybe it'll help them gain more funding. Not that *Brio* readers have a lot of money to spare."

"She should do a photo shoot here at the ranch," Becca said.

"It's already being planned."

Solana wrapped her arms around herself and watched the evening sky. A sense of peace came over her. No way would she let herself be upset with things not working out exactly like she'd wanted. She looked at her friends. "I couldn't have done this without you guys. Thanks again for all your help."

Hannah smiled up at Solana from her place on the ground. Her blue eyes sparkled in the evening shade. "We did the easy parts." She hopped up. "Oh Solana, I forgot. I have a whole roll of pictures for you at home—for that photo album that Jacie was going to help you put together."

"That's right," Jacie said. "We never made the memory book." She shrugged. "I guess Solana doesn't need it now."

Solana glanced at her shoulder out of the corner of her eye. *I think I've found my perfect setting.* She ran her fingers over the tie on the light short-sleeved jacket she'd worn over her sundress. "Actually, I've got my own remembrance of the ranch." She untied the jacket and let it slip off her shoulders, turning her body to reveal the small multicolored dragonfly tattoo flying across her shoulder.

Becca gasped. "Solana! Oh my gosh!"

"You really did it." Jacie reached out to touch the tattoo. "Hey." She stepped back, pouting. "I wanted to design it."

"You can design one for Hannah." Solana grinned.

"In your dreams." Hannah swatted Solana.

Solana studied her friends' faces, trying to guess what they were thinking. "So, are you shocked?"

"No," Jacie and Becca said together.

Tyler eyed the tattoo more closely. "What shocks me is that you managed to hide it for so long."

"We should have suspected when she stopped wearing tank tops," Jacie whispered to Becca.

Solana turned to Hannah, who couldn't seem to take her eyes off the tattoo. "Okay, you. I know you're dying to comment. Say what's on your mind." She stuck out her shoulder. "Want to touch it? It won't bite."

Hannah reached out and touched the tattoo hesitantly. "Didn't it hurt?"

"Yes!" Solana shivered recalling the pain.

"It's . . ." Hannah pulled her hand back. "It's nice."

"*Nice?*" She smiled sarcastically at Becca. "My tattoo is nice."

Hannah stomped her foot in playful frustration. "Oh, you know what I'm trying to say. I mean, I wouldn't get one but it's . . . it's you."

Solana patted Hannah. "Good try."

Jacie stared at the tattoo for a moment. "When you think about it, this tattoo is perfect for you, Solana. It *is* you."

"It represents the ranch," Solana informed her, "and Dragonfly Pond."

"I know—but it also represents you."

Hannah, Becca, and Tyler examined the tattoo again, and then four pairs of eyes were on Solana. It was all she could do to keep from making a face at them.

Tyler smiled. "It *is* you."

Solana shook her head. "You guys are so weird."

Jacie's hands moved wildly as she started to explain. "A dragon-fly is quick and colorful, like you."

"They are also fragile," Tyler added. "And as much as you don't like to admit it, Solana, you are fragile."

Solana pretended to cry. "I know I am." She threw herself into Tyler's arms.

He pushed her away. "Oh, knock it off. You're ruining the moment."

Hannah's face beamed. "Dragonflies change."

"Remember how ugly that larva was when we watched it break out of its skin?" Jacie pointed out.

Solana scowled. "Thanks a lot!"

"Then," Jacie spoke over her, "it became something beautiful."

"And it took a long time to make that change," Becca pointed out. She looked sweetly into Solana's eyes. "I have a feeling that this is only the beginning. By the time we graduate, Stony Brook won't be able to recognize you."

Solana held her head high. "Yes. You have only seen a glimpse of my greatness." She put her arm around Becca. "Come on." She started toward the ranch. "Let's get back to the party before Ramón eats all the *carne asada*."

"By the way." Jacie added herself to Solana and Becca's chain. "It was fun having Ramón over last week. Bring him along more often."

"I will. I never thought I'd say this, but with a guy like Ramón, it's easier to date in a group. I don't think I need to explain why."

"I'm glad you're taking things slow," Hannah said.

"Well, we want to concentrate on school right now anyway. So, we'll see what happens."

"I bet you end up getting married," Jacie blurted out. She slapped her hand over her mouth. "Oops. Not what you want to hear I bet."

Solana laughed and pulled one of Jacie's curls.

"I have to admit," Becca said, "you are perfect for each other."

"So, can I sing at your wedding?" Tyler grabbed Solana's hand in both of his and pleaded. "I'll write a special song for the occa-

dragonfly on my shoulder

179

sion. It'll be really good. I figure I have at least five years to work on it."

Jacie, Hannah, and Becca laughed out loud.

"Well, let's not jump ahead of ourselves." Solana stopped and turned to Tyler. "But *if* that day ever comes—yes, Tyler, you can sing at the wedding." She pointed a finger into his chest. "Nothing sappy."

"So 'One Hand, One Heart' from *West Side Story* is out of the question?"

Solana gagged.

● ● ●

"There she is." Manuel held his arm out to Solana. He grabbed her in a huge bear hug and kissed her on the cheek. He looked into her eyes and smiled. Seeing the tinge of sadness behind her uncle's smile, Solana's doubts returned.

Manuel squeezed Solana's arm. "I want to thank you for being such a sneaky, stubborn girl and going behind my back."

Solana pulled away from her uncle. "You're welcome—I guess."

"Because if it were not for that," Manuel pulled her back, "this would be a farewell party for the ranch instead of a celebration." He kissed her again on the other cheek. "*Te amo.*"

"*Te amo, Tio* Manuel."

Solana tried to read her uncle's eyes. "Are you really okay with losing Dragonfly Pond? I mean, if it hurts me . . ."

"Shh." Manuel put a finger over Solana's lips. "We are keeping the part of the ranch that is most important to us."

Solana smiled and nodded. If Manuel could handle the loss, she could too. They got to keep the horses, and most importantly, Manuel and Maricella's house. The *tesoros puros* could continue grazing and living on open pasture. And she had something to remind her of Dragonfly Pond—it would always be a part of her.

● ● ●

Ellie ducked under a bundle of balloons and colored ribbon. "Wow, your family sure knows how to throw a party. I'll forever have a picture in mind of little Alvaro, busting the *piñata*." She pulled a piece of ribbon out of her hair that had fallen from one of the balloons. "And you have such nice parents, Solana. I was just talking to them."

Solana handed Ellie a plastic cupful of punch. "Yeah, they're okay. I think I'll keep 'em."

To Solana, Ellie looked about 10 years younger in her bright-colored, loose-fitting dress, with her hair hanging free, and her eyes sparkling with fun.

"Hey, can I pull you away from the punch for a sec?" Ellie headed for the porch. She moved someone's purse off the porch swing and sat, patting the place beside her. "I have something else for you to celebrate. At least I hope you will."

"What?" Solana sat.

"Remember when I told you that I wanted to hire an intern as an assistant?"

"Did you find one?"

"Well, yes." Ellie set her cup on a small table by the swing and folded her hands in her lap. "I've talked to everyone at the office and it's unanimous—we'd like to hire you."

Solana's mouth fell open. "Me?"

"I can't think of a better person. It's a paid position—maybe not enough money to brag about, but hey, it beats flipping burgers."

"Yeah it does!" Solana noticed that her hands were flailing around helplessly, in the same pathetic way that Hannah's often did. She clutched them together. A job, working for a conservancy—it seemed too good to be true. She reached out and hugged Ellie. "Thank you so much."

"Does this mean you accept?"

"Yes, I accept! Are you kidding?"

Tyler and Jacie ran up the porch steps. Tyler fell into a lounge chair. "So, what's going on?"

Jacie pulled up a folding chair. "Come on—share."

Solana looked at Ellie.

"It's your news." Ellie retrieved her punch, taking a sip.

Solana hopped up and yelled over the edge of the porch. "Becca, Hannah, Ramón—come here!" She blew exaggerated kisses at the party guests who turned their heads when she shouted. When the threesome reached the edge of the steps she waved them her way, her patience running out. "You'll never believe this—"

● ● ●

It was after midnight but Solana felt too excited to sleep. She sat at her desk writing furiously in her journal. Her pen could barely keep up with her thoughts.

> I can't believe all that has happened. It keeps getting better all the time. I've gone over and over it in my mind, trying to prove that it was just an amazing coincidence, but the ending is too perfect for that. I hate it when that happens! Then I have to admit that there is a slight chance that my friends could be right.
>
> So, if God did work all of this out, why would He do such a thing for me? Especially since I'm still not sure what to do with Him yet.
>
> I'm sure that it makes my friends very happy that I will be working for a Christian. I saw Hannah wink at Becca when I told them about my job. I

ignored it. I can see them all now, huddled in Jacie's shack.

"Oh, this is so from God!"

"I'm sure it's part of His plan."

"Praise the Lord!"

"Let's pray right now."

Like Ellie and I will have all kinds of extra time on our hands to sit around talking about spiritual things. We will be far too busy saving wildlife.

There is one thing I'm curious about—I won't admit this to my friends of course. Being an intelligent woman, Ellie surely thought about her decision before accepting faith in Christ. I wonder what finally sold her on it. Maybe I'll ask her sometime. MAYBE!

Who knows? With Ellie on my side, I might even get into Berkeley. This summer was crazy, but it's pretty amazing how everything worked out. As for Ramón—we'll see what happens. ☺

Check Out Focus on the Family's

The Christy Miller Series

Teens across the country adore Christy Miller! She has a passion for life, but goes through a ton of heart-wrenching circumstances. Though the series takes you to a fictional world, it gives you plenty of "food for thought" on how to handle tough issues as they come up in your own life!

The Ultimate Baby-Sitter's Survival Guide

Want to become everyone's favorite baby-sitter? This book is packed with practical information. It also features an entire section of safe, creative and downright crazy indoor and outdoor activities that will keep kids challenged, entertained and away from the television.

Sierra Jensen Series

The best-selling author of "The Christy Miller Series" leads you through the adventures of Sierra Jensen as she faces the same issues that you do as a teen today. You'll devour every exciting story, and she'll inspire you to examine your own life and make a deeper commitment to Christ!

Mind Over Media: The Power of Making Sound Entertainment Choices

You can't escape the ideas and images that come from the media, but you *can* weed through the bad and grasp the good! This video uses an exciting, MTV-style production to dissolve the misconceptions people have about the media. The companion book uses humor, questions, facts and stories to help you take charge of what enters your mind and then directs your actions.

Life on the Edge—Live!

This award-winning national radio call-in show gives teens like you something positive to tune in to every Saturday night. You'll get a chance to talk about the hottest issues of your generation—no topic is off-limits! See if it airs in your area by visiting us on the Web at www.lifeontheedgelive.com

Cool Stuff on Hot Topics!

My Truth, Your Truth, Whose Truth?

Who's to say what's right and wrong? This book shatters the myth that everything is relative and shows you the truth about absolute truth! It *does* matter…and is found only in Christ! Understand more about this hot topic in the unique video *My Truth, Your Truth, Whose Truth?*

No Apologies: The Truth About Life, Love and Sex

Read the truth about sex—the side of the story Hollywood doesn't want you to hear—in this incredible paperback featuring teens who've made decisions about premarital sex. You'll learn you're worth the wait. Discover more benefits of abstinence in the video *No Apologies: The Truth About Life, Love and Sex.*

Brio

Captivating fiction, real-life dramas, informative articles, devotions and godly advice columns await you in each issue—not to mention in-depth interviews with your favorite Christian artists. One-year subscription (12 issues).

Brio & Beyond

Brio & Beyond brings a Christian perspective to tough issues faced specifically by high school upperclassmen and college students. One-year subscription (12 issues).

Dare 2 Dig Deeper Girl's Package

Have you been looking for info on the issues you deal with? Yeah, that's what we thought. So we put some together for you from our popular "Dare 2 Dig Deeper" booklets with topics that are for girls only, such as: friendship, sexual abuse, eating disorders and purity. Set includes: *"Beyond Appearances," "A Crime of Force," "Fantasy World," "Forever, Friends," "Hold On to Your Heart"* and *"What's the Alternative?"*